The House of Hope

The House of Hope

Audrey Willsher

ROBERT HALE · LONDON

© Audrey Willsher 2011
First published in Great Britain 2011

ISBN 978-0-7090-9201-8

Robert Hale Limited
Clerkenwell House
Clerkenwell Green
London EC1R 0HT

www.halebooks.com

2 4 6 8 10 9 7 5 3 1

Typeset in 11/15½pt Sabon
Printed in the UK by the MPG Books Group,
Bodmin and King's Lynn

To Rosemary and Jean with thanks for all your help and encouragement.

Chapter One

1946

'Stretton Magna, your stop, m'dook,' the conductor called down the bus. He waited for Marianne to step on to the pavement, then handed over her suitcase. 'Peculiar place this,' he observed with a shake of his head.

Since the man had called into question the sanity, honesty and parentage of the inhabitants of just about every village they'd driven through, Marianne ignored the remark. It was directions she was after, not pointless village gossip. 'Do you by any chance happen to know the way to Hope Grange?' she asked with excessive politeness.

'Hope Grange?' The conductor scratched his chin. 'I dunno. Memory like a sieve, me. Nope, sorry, it don't ring a bell, but there in't that many houses, so you shouldn't have any trouble finding it,' he offered by way of encouragement.

'Thanks. *For nothing*,' Marianne added under her breath.

'Take care now.'

'Don't worry, I will.'

'A young girl on her own …' The words left unsaid carried a weight of meaning.

He dinged the bell, Marianne returned his wave, then watched the bus disappear into a wet, fading autumn afternoon. Gripped by a sense of abandonment, she pulled up the hood of her waterproof – coupon-free from an army surplus store – and studied her surroundings. The village had a closed-in, secretive air and the only sound was rain gurgling along the gutter, the only movement a single leaf spiralling to the ground. God, what a dump! A creepy one, too. 'It's all your bloomin' fault, Renée, marrying that Chuck,' Marianne accused her absent aunt and was about to move on when she noticed fire-wood stacked high in the middle of the green. Of course, it would soon be bonfire night. Only it wasn't Guy Fawkes awaiting his annual roasting. Curious, Marianne moved closer and saw that the figure skewered to the summit wore skirts, and that rope curls peeped out from an old-fashioned bonnet. And the poor creature's head seemed to loll in despair while her mouth was a slash of black ink. A crude representation of a pair of red shoes had also been painted on to her feet, and Marianne glanced down at her own shoes with a sense of disquiet, for they were the same blood-red. She shivered and for a second she had the strangest feeling of being caught between two worlds. '*Stop it*!' Marianne rubbed her temples fretfully. It was lack of food and tiredness that were making her light-headed. 'You are in Stretton Magna,' she reminded herself, 'you need to reach Hope Grange before it gets dark, There's the main road, so get a move on.'

But as she squelched across the waterlogged grass Marianne was aware of an oozing dampness between her toes. When she reached the hard-surfaced road, she stared down at her shoes with dismay. All that money and all those coupons and look at them: ruined. Oh why hadn't she bought sensible brogues, like she'd intended? Because of her grandmother, of course. Although all that remained of *her* was her spirit; that ghostly voice was always there in her head, nagging, guiding, and that day it had been particularly insistent. 'For lawd's sake, what's got into you? They're old ladies' shoes,' she'd scolded, immediately changing her tune when the salesgirl brought over the red shoes. 'Now those *are* smart.'

And Nan had been right. For six years the world had been khaki-coloured and she was entitled to spoil herself, put a bit of cheerfulness back in her life. The shoes would dry out, polish up. Reassured by her own logic, but taking care to avoid the potholes, Marianne set off along Stocks Lane.

A pub – closed, she discovered – the village hall, a row of labourers' cottages and a primitive wattle-and-daub dwelling straggled out along its length and soon the road petered out into a cinder track. Here Marianne found her way barred by a gate.

In front of her endless fields stretched into the misty distance and on the horizon a ploughman and his team of horses were turning over the sodden earth. And that was it. The edge of the world. To assure herself that she had come to the right place Marianne pulled a letter from her coat pocket. Set out in it were her terms of employment: thirty shillings a week in wages, every Saturday afternoon off, plus a week's annual holiday. It all sounded promising enough except in one particular; Hugo Lacey Esq had failed to send her directions, which made her think that her future employer must be elderly and a bit absent-minded, or just plain thoughtless. Neither prospect was encouraging.

Did she go north, south, east or west? Marianne gave a dispirited sigh. She had to face up to it; she was lost. To think that today was meant to be a new start, yet here she was in this misbegotten place and already beset by doubts and problems.

She was retracing her steps when she heard voices. Through a gap in the hedge Marianne spotted a gang of men bent low, cutting cabbages. They looked as wet and dejected as she did but it raised her spirits just to see a human face. She was about to call out for directions, when one of the men glanced up and smiled at her.

'Hello,' said Marianne, encouraged by his friendly manner.

'*Guten Tag.*' The man inclined his head.

The unfamiliar phrase momentarily threw Marianne but then she noticed his dark-brown uniform and the telltale patch. A German prisoner of war, one of her nan's killers! How dare the man even look at her, never mind speak to her. 'Nazi!' she hissed, not quite under her breath, and he must have heard, because his expression became defensive. He bent and picked up a sack of cabbages, slung it across his shoulder and strode off down the row.

Hatred slewed Marianne's stomach and she turned away, all the misery of her loss stirred up again at the sight of the young German. Although it was over two years since a V2 rocket had destroyed their house in Camberwell and killed her grandmother Marianne was still in mourning for her. And as if her nan's death hadn't been enough to cope with, after meeting Chuck in Trafalgar Square on VE night, her aunt Renée had sailed off to the land of plenty as a GI bride. As they clung to each other at Waterloo station there'd been tears by the gallon, promises by the yard, but although her aunt was generous with the nylons and Hershey bars, that promise to send for her once she was settled turned out to be pie in the sky. She would never set foot in America and was stuck here for ever in this dreary war-torn country.

Marianne's throat tightened in pity at her orphan state; she was so absorbed in the wretchedness of her existence she'd almost gone past the wattle-and-daub house before she noticed the large square window, empty apart from a rusting Oxo tin and a half-empty jar of liquorice torpedoes. Above the window a faded sign read: E Hardcastle Purveyor of Quality Foods.

Half-expecting the shop to be closed, Marianne tried the handle. To her surprise, the door swung open and she found herself stepping down into a dark, low-ceilinged room that smelt of soap, cheese and candle wax. A tall, sallow-faced woman stood guard over rows of dusty shelves and although her eyes were barely visible beneath their warty flaps, Marianne was aware of being assessed.

'We're out of bread if that's what you've come for. No more deliveries until tomorrow.'

The woman's manner was churlish, but Marianne almost welcomed it because it snapped her out of her self-pity and back to the real world of austerity and food shortages. She dropped her suitcase, pushed back the hood of her waterproof and ran her fingers through her short brown curls. 'It's not bread I'm after, thank you, but directions.'

'Where to?' the woman asked grudgingly.

'Hope Grange.' Marianne gave the shopkeeper her best smile.

'What d'you want to go to that place for?'

'I have a position there.'

The shopkeeper looked interested. 'Have you now. What as?'

The advertisement in *The Lady* magazine had been for a domestic help with some plain cooking, and she apparently fitted the bill, although she didn't consider this any of old nosy parker's business. Marianne picked up her suitcase. 'It seems you can't help me so I'll be on my way.'

'If you had any sense, you'd catch the next bus out,' the shop-keeper called after her.

Marianne was so taken aback she dropped her suitcase again. 'Why should I do that?'

Miss Hardcastle shrugged. 'Well, the last bus 'as gone anyway so you best continue on down Stocks Lane, then cut through the churchyard. That'll bring you out on to Fosse Lane, which'll take you to where you want to go. It's a bit of a walk, but you won't miss it, because there in't another house around for miles.'

Marianne managed a thank you, reached the door and paused. 'The figure on the bonfire – I noticed it's a woman. Unusual, that.'

'Not in these parts.'

'Oh. Why?'

'Because she were a witch and they burn her each year as a punishment for what she done.'

Marianne's curiosity quickened. 'And what was that?'

'She cast spells, bewitched men. There wa' no end to that critter's wickedness.'

These country-folk, they were still in the Dark Ages with their superstitions. 'So when was this supposed to have happened?'

'Oh, a hundred years ago.'

'And they're still punishing her?'

'Folks don't forget easy round here. And you always want to remember that,' the woman warned darkly.

Marianne bristled at the imputation. 'Well, I'll have you know I came here by bus and train, not on a broomstick.'

'Never said you did.'

'Bad-tempered old trout.' Marianne closed the door forcefully. That was the trouble with food shortages and rationing, it turned shopkeepers into little Hitlers.

The clock was striking five as Marianne reached the church and made her way along the path between the gravestones. As if they'd timed it there was a sudden whirring of wings as hundreds of starlings swooped in to settle down for the night on gushing waterspouts with their leering gargoyle faces. Marianne's spine tingled and she couldn't help but be reminded of the many horror films she'd watched with fearful delight through half-open fingers. And wasn't it about now in the plot that the graves opened and the dead came crawling out? Her instinct was to run, instead she forced herself to pause and read the headstones, many half-sunk in the ground or leaning this way and that like badly aligned teeth.

One name brought her up short. The headstone was of slate and shiny with rain, making it hard to decipher the words chipped out by the mason's chisel. Leaning closer, Marianne read the dedication. 'Here lies the body of Hugo Lacey, Gentleman, died November 1846 cut down by a woman in the full flower of his manhood. The debt he owed was small to cost him his life but God in his vengeance this woman will pursue until she meets an equal fate.'

Marianne took a step back and in spite of her resolve, the name, the chill atmosphere, the possibility of murder, took such a hold on her imagination that when something batlike flickered in the corner of her eye, she reacted with a squeak of terror.

But it was only the vicar striding towards her. 'Good afternoon, can I be of assistance?'

Conscious that she must look like orphan Annie, Marianne stuttered, 'No ... thank you, I'm on my way to Hope Grange. I have employment there.'

The vicar studied her with interest. 'Oh, have you? He pointed to the far end of the churchyard. 'Well you'll find it through that gate.'

She expected him to be watching her, but when she turned to close the gate light was illuminating the stained glass in the lancet windows. It was a rather comforting sight and Marianne was tempted to turn back, go in and sit down.

But knowing she had to reach her destination before dark, Marianne set off along the lane and was soon in open country with a bitter wind blowing wind in her face. Her last meal had been a sausage roll and cup of stewed tea in the station buffet and her stomach gave a protesting rumble. In the distance she heard the rattle of a train and wished she were on it heading back to London. But what to? That job she'd had in the paper factory and detested? No thanks.

Marianne was beginning to wonder whether she might be on another futile tramp when she saw ahead a chimney rising from a clump of trees. Keeping it in her sights, she hurried towards it. Pillars marked the entrance, but the gates they'd once supported had collapsed into the undergrowth and lay like rusting bones. However, the words Hope Grange, picked out in wrought iron, told her all she needed to know.

'Thank God.' Her future decided, Marianne flexed her aching arms, turned into a dark void of arching trees and paused. There was a rustling of leaves and she tensed. 'This is the last lap, keep going,' she urged her weary body and was about to move on when a violent blow to the chest, sent her reeling. 'What the hell...?' As she struggled to right herself, she was struck again, this time on the face. Clawing the air in panic, Marianne let out a scream, which reverberated around the rain-lashed countryside.

'Kindly stop making that din!' a voice admonished from somewhere above her head, then a light was shone in her face and Marianne saw, swinging in front of her, the stuffed effigy of a woman. A rope was secured round her neck and her feet were red daubs of paint.

'Oh no!' Marianne recoiled in horror and nausea swirled around in her stomach.

'That frightened you, didn't it?' The voice was young, gleeful.

Certain now that some evil spirit stalked the countryside, Marianne had to force herself to look up. Her tormentor lay sprawled along the branch of a tree, but in the uncertain light of the torch, his features were ghostly, the eye-sockets black, and to Marianne, he looked more like a malevolent hobgoblin than the small boy she could now see he was.

'What do you think you're up to, you vile beast?'

'Putting the wind up you for keeping me waiting. You are the new maid, I assume?'

'None of your business.' Marianne drew a handkerchief from her pocket and dabbed her nose. 'And see what you've done, made me nose bleed.'

The boy scrambled down from the tree and shone the torch in her face. 'So I have.' He smirked.

Marianne's last vestige of control vanished and she grabbed him by the collar. 'I'll wring your neck if you're not careful,' she threatened.

'Lemmee go!' the boy hollered and landed her one on the shins. Quick as lightning Marianne's hand shot out and gave him a slap across the face. Then, feeling honour had been satisfied, she picked up her suitcase.

'Do you know who I am?' the boy called as Marianne stumbled through numerous potholes.

'No, and I don't care.'

'I am Master Gerald Lacey.'

There was a danger now that her legs would buckle under her. He had to be bluffing; he was a servant's child. Not with those cut-glass vowels.

He overtook her and drew himself up to his full height of three foot and a bit. 'And just you wait. When my father gets home, you'll be in for it.'

'And what about your high jinks eh? I think he'll be very interested to hear about that.'

'No, don't say anything, please. I won't snitch on you, if you don't snitch on me, I promise.'

'OK.' Surprised by his conciliatory tone, Marianne thought: so the little thug's frightened of his pa, is he? In the event of a further outbreak of hostilities it was useful information to have.

'Anyway, you'd better follow me. Grandmama sent me out to look for you and I've been waiting ages.' Gerald set off, walking some way in front. The stuffed doll was tucked under his arm and although the legs dangled ludicrously, Marianne couldn't rid herself of the notion that it was somehow human.

'So, Master Gerald, you think yourself something of a gentleman, do you?' Marianne challenged.

'There's no think about it, I am. The Lacey family has occupied this house for over three hundred years.'

'I hope they were more welcoming to strangers than you are.'

'You shouldn't have been so late.'

'And you shouldn't be so lippy,' Marianne snapped. By now the drive had opened up to reveal a house. But no welcoming lights shone from its windows; mock battlements gave it an impregnable look and Marianne's first impression was of something large and grim.

'Tradesmen's entrance for you,' Gerald called. He marched on round to the side of the house and pushed open a door. 'The kitchen,' he announced.

Marianne dropped her suitcase and waited for a welcoming rush of warmth. Instead she was greeted by the dank chill of unlit fires and cold water.

She shivered; then, without thinking, exclaimed, 'God, it's cold enough to freeze the balls off a brass monkey in here.'

Gerald laughed and switched on the light. A bulb of extremely low wattage sent out such a feeble glow that most of the room remained in shadow. However she did notice a large, unlit range, with sticks and coal beside it. I'll soon have that going, she thought and was about to remove her coat when Gerald said, 'You've to come with me.' He marched her up some stairs and along a corridor hung with paintings of long-departed Laceys and slaughtered animals. Gerald knocked at a door and a voice inside barked, 'Enter.'

He walked on in but Marianne, overcome with nerves, paused on the threshold. The smell that hit her nostrils was of old skin and old clothes. A four-poster bed hung with moth-eaten drapes dominated the room, and piles of yellowing newspapers lapped against the feet of a woman sitting by an empty grate. She wore a dress that might have been fashionable in Queen Victoria's time, and a black-bead choker supported her neck.

'Don't stand there like a lamppost, girl. Come in,' the woman snapped, beckoning with a mittened hand. The room had little to offer in the way of comfort, but there was heating in the form of a cylinder-shaped paraffin stove, and a fuggy warmth spilled out through its fretwork design. The woman pointed with her stick to a chair. 'Sit.' She might have been addressing a dog.

No need to waste time liking you then, m'lady, Marianne decided.

Grandma banged her walking-stick to gain Marianne's attention. 'You are late, young woman.'

'I'm sorry, madam, but I got lost.' *Trying to find this god-forsaken place.* 'I wasn't sent any directions.'

'You've got a tongue in your head, haven't you?' Her eyes were pale and watery like pebbles in a pond.

Explaining, Marianne suspected, would be a waste of breath. Instead she glowered. She wasn't staying here to be treated like a doormat. She'd get her first week's wages and be off. There were plenty of people looking for domestics; you only had to open a newspaper to know that. More at ease with herself, Marianne folded herself comfortably into the chair and watched the old woman wrap wire spectacles round her ears and study her letter of application.

'You give your name as Marianne.'

'Yes with two ens and an ee.'

'A bit fanciful for a girl of your type.'

Marianne ignored the insult. 'I was called after me nan.' Or if she was going to be strictly truthful, Mary like her nan. An honourable name but plain nevertheless. So plain that she'd been Marianne in her head for quite a while now. However, sensing her work-mates were probably not quite ready for such an exotic name she'd waited until she boarded the train at St Pancras this morning to make it official.

The woman sniffed. 'Well, I shall call you Armstrong anyway. Now tell me, are young women with fancy names able to light kitchen ranges?'

'If there's enough coal and sticks, madam.'

'Right. Gerald, show Armstrong to her room.'

'Follow me,' the boy ordered. He marched Marianne up a narrow, uncarpeted staircase to a sparsely furnished room under the eaves. Marianne gazed about her with dismay. Every object in the room had a crack in it; the jug on the washstand, the mirror, the linoleum. The wind had reached gale force and the branches of a tree tapped eerily against the casement. Thank God for Renée's hot-water bottle, pressed on her with the words, 'Take it, duckie, I'll have me love to keep me warm from now on.' Oh Auntie, where are you when I need you? In blinkin' Pittsburg, that's where.' Tears of loneliness began to slide down Marianne's cheeks.

'What are you crying for?' Gerald moved closer, peering up at her.

Marianne turned away and made a great exercise of pulling the water bottle from her case. 'I'm not crying. It's the cold, it always makes me eyes water. Isn't there anyone in this house capable of lighting a fire?'

'Yes. My father.'

'So where is he?' Marianne had taken it for granted that her employer would be here to greet her when she arrived.

'He's still in the army and only comes home at the weekend.'

In the army, eh? Well that took care of the elderly and absent-minded employer, which left, rather worryingly, the thoughtless one.

'Anyway it's a servant's job to light fires,' Gerald pointed out.

'Have they all got the day off, then?' Marianne asked.

'Who?'

'The other servants.'

'There's only you.'

'Are you telling me I've got to run this great pile on my own?' Gerald nodded.

But not for long, Sunny Jim. 'Have you eaten today?'

'I had dinner at school and some bread and jam when I came in.'

'Lucky you.' Marianne studied the boy. He wasn't under-fed but, like the house, there was an air of dusty neglect about him, as if no one bothered to check that his neck was clean, his hair and shoes brushed before he went to school. 'Is there any food at all in this house?' The prospect of going to bed hungry began to loom worryingly.

'There's some eggs.'

'You mean real eggs with shells on, and not that dried stuff?'

'Of course.'

It was the most encouraging bit of news Marianne had heard all day and she had a fire going in no time at all. Gerald immediately sat down and pulled off his shoes. Marianne saw that he had holes as large as potatoes in the heels of his socks.

'Well, are you going to cook something, then?' he asked in that snotty-nosed tone of his.

'When you've told me where the food is.'

'Over there, in the larder.'

Marianne followed his pointing finger to a cupboard and found, lying on a slate shelf, a dozen speckled brown eggs, half a loaf, margarine, milk and tea, which if not exactly a feast, was enough to be going on with. She put the kettle on to boil, laid a tray for Mrs Lacey and boiled two eggs for her supper. Since she probably hadn't eaten all day, Marianne expected a word of thanks at the very least. Instead the old lady studied the eggs critically; then, without a word, peeled the shell off one and sank her spoon into it. Done to a turn, thought Marianne as the yolk oozed down the sides.

'Too hard,' Mrs Lacey announced.

'Shall I take them away, madam?' Marianne bent to remove the tray, but for an elderly person, Mrs Lacey had a strong grip and she wouldn't let it go. 'I'd better eat them, I suppose.' She sighed. 'Now go. I don't like being stared at while I'm eating.'

Marianne held her tongue and marched back to the kitchen. Here she found the doll in a chair by the fire, as if it were part of the family. But she was in no mood for Gerald's games. 'Move that thing, now,' she ordered and went and poured herself a cup of tea.

'Annie's thirsty; she wants a cup of tea, too.'

'It's been a long day and I've had enough of your nonsense. Either you get it out of my sight or you go to bed supperless.' Hands on hips, Marianne waited.

Gerald considered her proposition, then picked up the doll and left. When he returned, Marianne asked, 'Now how do you want your eggs, boiled or fried?'

'Fried.'

'Trying saying please.'

Gerald gave her an old fashioned look. 'Please.'

'Who cooked for you before?'

'Someone from the village.'

'And what happened to her?'

'She left.' Then to save Marianne the trouble of asking, he added, 'And the one before that.'

And little do you know that I won't be far behind, thought Marianne, and felt a brief sympathy for the boy. Here he was alone in this bleak house with only his sour old grandmother for company. Marianne slid the eggs on to a plate and set them down on the table. So where was his mother?

The cause of her concern was now shovelling the food into his mouth. Watching him Marianne thought, well for all their airs and graces, no one has bothered to teach him table manners. 'Where do you go to school, Master Gerald?'

Gerald wiped the plate clean with a piece of bread, gulped down the rest of his tea and held out the cup for a refill. 'In the village. But I don't like it. The other children are so uncouth. I was down for Eton, but with all his other expenses, Father decided he couldn't afford it.' He yawned widely.

'You look ready for bed. Shall I fill a hot-water bottle for you?' Marianne asked.

'Hot-water bottles are for sissies.'

'Who says so?'

'My father.' Gerald stood up and pushed back his chair. 'Will you make my breakfast in the morning?'

'That's what I'm here for. What time do you want it?'

'Half past seven.'

'And your grandmother?'

'She'll ring. She always has it in bed with *The Times*. G'night Armstrong.'

When he'd gone, Marianne refilled the teapot and kicked off her shoes. The red dye had run and her toes looked like sausages. But the fire was burning well, and she sat with her feet resting on the fender, mulling over the past few hours. To think that this time yesterday she'd been full of optimism, imagining that returning to Leicestershire would put her life back on course.

And look where she'd ended up. Marianne gazed around the dreary kitchen. Her bedsit in Camberwell had been more comfortable than this. A shame her landlady had wanted it for her son, recently demobbed and about to get married. It showed that it never did to expect too much from life, because it was always going to bop you one on the nose just to let you know who was boss. Marianne finished her tea, put the plates and cutlery into the sink, added a handful of soda, and then turned on the tap. They could soak until morning. She banked up the fire, checked that the back door was secure, filled her hot-water bottle and, hugging it to her chest, climbed the stairs to her room.

Marianne fumbled around in the dark for the switch, found it, then stepped back with a shriek. For the bare bulb fell like a spotlight on to the stuffed doll straddling the bed, and its slit of a mouth seemed to be grinning at her malevolently.

'That little so and so … wait till I get him …' Anger and fear churning around in her stomach, Marianne grabbed the creature by its legs and hurled it down the narrow stairs. It thumped to a stop and lay there, the painted red feet pointing towards her. Convinced the doll would come in the night and take possession of her soul, Marianne slammed shut the door and, with trembling fingers, turned the key in the lock.

Chapter Two

Shrieking, 'He's here! He's here! My father's coming up the drive,' Gerald fell through the door and galloped round the kitchen like a red Indian on the warpath.

'For heaven's sake, do you have to make such a racket?' Marianne snapped, already nervous enough.

Gerald stopped and faced her across the table. 'It's my house and I'll do what I want.'

'And it's my kitchen and you won't,' Marianne shot back.

Gerald scowled at her. 'I'm going to tell my father to sack you.'

'What, again? But I suggest you wait until he's had his dinner. And if you don't mind I'd like to get on with it.'

Gerald gave a shrug and swaggered off, leaving Marianne to continue paunching and skinning a rabbit that would be their dinner. She was expecting her employer to walk through the door at any moment and nerves made her clumsy. What would he make of her? With more blood on her hands than a murderer, she certainly didn't look her best, although on the plus side it would prove that she was industrious and worth her wages.

Over these past few days Marianne had tried to build up a picture of her employer, wavering between an older version of Gerald and younger version of his mother, or even a combination of the two, God help him. Well, there was only one way to find out. Marianne slung the rabbit's entrails on to a piece of newspaper, rinsed her hands, went to the door, checked that the coast was clear and shot up the stairs to the first landing. Here a huge square window decorated with heraldic panels of stained glass gave Marianne a perfect view over the front of the house. She was in time to see a small sports car pull up and Gerald rush forward and wrestle with the handle.

'Hello Daddy,' Marianne heard him say in an unusually respectful tone as a tall man in an army officer's uniform stepped out on to the gravel and eased his shoulders with several circular movements. Marianne craned forward to get a better look, noting dark hair and regular features. And there was no missing the arrogant slant of the mouth, for it dominated his face. Even more noticeable was his lack of warmth towards his son. In fact he barely gave him a glance. Instead, in a sergeant-major voice, he barked, 'Bring my suitcase, Gerald,' and disappeared into the porch, while the boy struggled after him with the heavy case.

All right, Gerald was hardly endearing, but he was Hugo Lacey's only child and usually only children were loved to bits. She had been anyway. But there were different ways of showing love, she supposed. It could be that he was besotted with his son but uncomfortable with public displays of affection. Men often were.

Downstairs she heard the studded oak door creak open. Sensing that her employer would take a dim view of a domestic servant giving him the once-over, she slipped back to the kitchen. By the time the door slammed shut she was hacking away at the rabbit as if she'd never been away.

It was Miss Webb who'd taught her all her domestic skills as well as how to cast off her south London accent and talk properly. Although it hadn't always been the case, she now looked back on the years she was evacuated with the spinster lady with a sense of gratitude. In the beginning, though, Miss Webb had been an unwilling foster parent and she, at twelve, a reluctant evacuee. Worse, with Aunt Renée in the ATS, she'd had to leave her nan behind in Camberwell to face the blitz alone. How she cried on the train, and then she'd found herself stuck in the wilds of Leicestershire with an elderly woman who, it seemed to Marianne, had more to say to her chickens than she did to her new charge.

'Anyway it's thanks to me that the family are having this,' Marianne reminded herself as, with one clean stroke, she decapitated the rabbit. As the head rolled across the board, she indulged herself by imagining it was Mrs Lacey's, for the old lady constantly set out to humiliate her. Like yesterday, for instance, when she'd gone to ask her for a few shillings for meat. 'Get the butcher to put it on our account,' she'd answered, in her usual dismissive tone.

But Mr Veal, the butcher, was having none of it. After establishing who she was, he'd enquired, 'And how are you paying for this liver, me dook?'

'Mrs Lacey says you're to put it on the account.'

'Sorry, cash only.' Although he was halfway through weighing the offal, the butcher slid it back on to the tray. 'No more credit for the Laceys. Last month's bill in't bin settled yet.'

There was a queue of women behind Marianne and her skin reddened. 'I'm sorry, I didn't realize, I've only just started working there, you see,' she mumbled.

'T'int your fault, m'dook. But you just go back and tell that old biddy from me that I want that bill paid today. Then she can have her liver.'

Her head bowed in shame Marianne scurried out of the shop, a buzz of voices following her as if she were responsible for the Lacey debts. She leapt on the bicycle she'd discovered in an outhouse and pedalled home at top speed. She still needed meat, offal wasn't rationed, and if she didn't look smart it would be sold out. She reached the house, flung down the bike and raced upstairs to the old lady's room. Mrs Lacey was doing *The Times* crossword and she looked up with an irritable frown.

'What is it, Armstrong? And do stop panting!'

Cow! But I'll show her. 'Mr Veal says this family will not get an ounce of meat from him until you've paid him what he's owed, madam.'

Marianne watched her mouth tighten, the pebble eyes shoot out shards of ice. But the old lady belonged to that breed who despised the lower orders and she quickly went on the attack. 'That man is an unspeakable little upstart! Yet before the war he was grateful for any custom the Laceys gave him. He'll have to wait. I have no money.'

This was alarming news. 'What about me wages?' Marianne blurted out.

'My son deals with all the money matters; speak to him tomorrow.'

'But there's still lunch on Saturday and there's no food in the house except eggs.'

'Catch one of the chickens and wring its neck.'

'Me?' Marianne squeaked.

'Yes, you.'

'That's not part of my duties. It'll have to be eggs again.' But even Marianne was getting tired of a diet of eggs, so when an old tramp came to the back door later that morning and offered her the rabbit for sixpence, Marianne paid up, no questions asked.

She finished cutting up vegetables and added them to the stew-pot along with some parsley and a bay leaf picked from a tree in the garden, and left it to simmer on the hob.

Miss Webb had also taught her how to raise pastry over a mould to make a pork pie and how to make bread. In the autumn they had gone foraging for nuts and mushrooms, gathered blackberries from the hedgerows, which she transformed into a sweet dark wine and put to join the bottled fruit on the pantry shelf.

The saucepan lid began to rattle and an aroma of herbs and vegetables filled the kitchen. Marianne gave it a stir, then began beating the eggs for a baked egg custard.

On the day after her arrival Marianne had gone exploring the grounds and had found, among the crumbling, ivy-covered statuary, a run with hens scratching around in it. There was also an apple tree with a few apples still clinging to its branches. 'I can do something with those,' she said to herself and went in search of a ladder. She found one in the stables and as she stood there, the weirdest thing happened. She heard a clatter and ghosts of the past came galloping into the yard: mud-splattered men in their blood-red coats, women in riding-habits, steaming horses, panting dogs, all sharing in the excitement of the kill. Then with a burst of laughter, they vanished, and all that remained was a broken door swinging on its hinges and an atmosphere of desolation and neglect. Marianne felt a cold breath on her cheeks and, as she shook her head to clear it of phantoms, high in the branches of an elm a crow cawed as if in warning. It was time to turn back. Too much of this and she would begin to doubt her sanity.

Slightly disorientated, Marianne pushed her way through the undergrowth, only realizing how large the grounds were when she came upon a dilapidated greenhouse. Further on was a lake, rank and dark and filled with weeds, on which a solitary moorhen paddled. *God, the whole place reeks of unhappiness and the sooner I escape the better.*

Noticing a few Michaelmas daisies and Chinese lanterns languishing in a flower-bed, Marianne picked them. An even pleasanter surprise was the discovery of a vegetable patch and she speculated on who could have planted it out. Certainly there was no gardener. Once, of course, there would have been battalions of them cultivating vegetables and nurturing exotic blooms for grand dinner parties. But the glory days had gone; only the ghosts remained and Marianne wondered what had brought about the sad decline in the family fortunes.

The vegetables and eggs proved to be a godsend and she was grating nutmeg on to the custard before placing it in the oven when, behind her, a male voice said, 'That smells absolutely delicious.'

Marianne closed the oven door and swung round. Hugo Lacey was advancing towards her. 'You will be Armstrong.' He smiled.

Ye … s, sir.' Marianne blushed, rubbed her palms down her apron and almost curtsied.

'May I ask what it is?'

'Rabbit stew with baked custard to follow.'

'And how long do I have to wait?'

'Luncheon will be served at one o'clock, Captain Lacey, in the dining room.' *Set the table for three*, had been the old lady's instructions. *And don't forget to sound the gong.* She had also been ordered to wax the dining-room table, polish the cutlery and wash the cobwebs out of cut-glass goblets. When she'd done setting the table, Marianne placed the posy of flowers she'd found in the garden in the centre, then stood back and surveyed her efforts with a sense of pride. She didn't expect anyone to notice, but it did look rather splendid. Pity that the dining room was an icebox, but Mrs Lacey had forbidden her to light a fire. Still, her food would warm them up.

'I look forward to it.' Hugo Lacey gave her another smile. 'And welcome to Hope Grange.'

'Thank you, sir,' Marianne replied, so diverted by broad shoulders and the way his hair sprang back from a pronounced widow's peak, that she briefly forgot she wouldn't be here after next week. In the meantime a bit of parade-ground discipline on his son wouldn't go amiss, because the misdeeds were piling up. The doll in the bed had been just one of a string of incidents; a live frog in her pocket another, worms on her dinner plate the last straw. Complaints to his grandmother were a waste of time, for in her eyes her grandson was a perfect little angel.

Later when Marianne went to clear the dining room she saw that the family had polished off every morsel of food, plus a whole bottle of wine. She picked up the bottle and studied the label. Margaux 1930. Marianne wasn't a drinker and all she knew about wine was that it was consumed by the wealthy. Still, it was a comfort to know that the Laceys had a bob or two to splash out on luxuries, because, as yet, no one had thought to pay her.

Deciding to keep the bottle, Marianne was about to rinse it out when she noticed that there was still a little wine left in it. Gingerly she lifted the bottle to her lips. She'd imagined a superior sort of lemonade, but the wine had a metallic taste and when it hit her throat she gave a splutter of disgust and spat it in to the sink. She was still draped over the sink when, to her dismay, she heard Hugo Lacey's voice.

'Armstrong, I've come to congratulate you on your cooking. It was an excellent meal, particularly in these times of austerity.'

Marianne hurriedly wiped her mouth with the back of her hand and spun round. 'Thank you sir.'

'Can I look forward to more? I'm home most weekends.'

Seduced by his compliments, Marianne began planning next week's menu in her head. Oxtail stew, he'd love that.

'And just one more request. As you probably know, it's Guy Fawkes night and they've got fireworks and a bonfire on the green. I was wondering whether you'd do me an enormous favour and take my son along?' Hugo Lacey glanced down at

Gerald, who was standing beside him with an unnaturally meek expression on his face. 'I would have gone with him myself, but unfortunately I have a rather pressing engagement.'

Now this was asking her to do something that went far beyond her domestic duties; it was also her afternoon off. But again her employer smiled and Marianne heard herself say, 'Of course I will, Captain Lacey.'

'Good. That's settled then. Say thank you to Armstrong, Gerald.'

'Thank you, Armstrong,' the boy repeated obediently, then spoiled it by showing Marianne the tip of his tongue.

After the praise and calls on her time, Marianne expected Hugo Lacey to take a roll of bank notes from his pocket and pay her. Instead he turned to leave. Not quite believing it, she let him reach the kitchen door before blurting out, 'Mr Lacey, what about my wages?'

He swung round. 'Wages?'

'Yes, Mrs Lacey said you would pay me today.'

'Oh yes, how much did I say?'

'Thirty shillings a week.'

He patted his jacket as if trying to remember where his wallet was. 'Ah ... I'm afraid I'm a little short at the moment. Could you possibly hold on until next week?'

'We ... ll, I don't know,' she answered feebly.

'Good. I promise you will have your wages next Saturday. You deserve every penny. It's a long time since we had good food in this house.'

'It's not only my wages. The butcher refused to serve me yesterday.'

'May I ask why?'

'Because last month's account hasn't been settled yet.'

'But why on earth hasn't my mother paid the wretched man?'

'She said you would deal with it when you came home.'

'Did she now.'

'Oh ... before you go, Mr Lacey, I'm owed sixpence for the rabbit. I paid for it out of my own pocket.'

By the set of his jaw-line, she could see he was struggling to contain his temper. He fumbled in his trouser pocket and slapped a silver coin on the table.

'Thank you, Armstrong, but there is no reason why you should be paying for our food. I give my mother a regular and adequate allowance to cover household expenses, so I will go and deal with the matter right away. I promise it won't happen again. I will also settle with Mr Veal.'

Marianne was drying the last plate when she heard the sound of a car engine. Hugo Lacey on his way to settle his debts and spare her any further humiliation, she hoped. She hung the tea towel to dry, made herself a cup of tea and sat down in front of the fire. At last a bit of time to herself. Marianne gave a sigh of pleasure and picked up a book. Yesterday while dusting the library she'd found a world atlas on one of the shelves. She pulled it out and looked up Pittsburg, then stared at the map of America with dismay. All that land, all that sea, Renée would never make it back home, the distances were too great. Feeling more abandoned than ever, she returned the atlas to its place and as she did so, she found, tucked behind a Latin primer, *Gone With The Wind*. She slipped it into her pocket.

Marianne took a sip of tea, opened the book and saw written on the fly-leaf in bold black ink, 'To my beloved Felicity, always and ever, Hugo,' Underneath was the date, July 1937. Marianne let the book fall to her lap. So that was her name. 'Felicity.' She said it out loud. Gerald's mother, Hugo Lacey's wife, these loving words the first proof of her existence. To think she'd held this book, read it. And she would have been beautiful, because men of Hugo Lacey's class only married beauties. But dead, she assumed. Poor Captain Lacey, poor motherless Gerald. No wonder the boy was difficult. She knew, as much as anyone, how it knocked your world sideways when you lost someone you loved. Resolving to make allowances in future, Marianne turned to chapter one.

Immediately she was captivated by headstrong Scarlett O'Hara and the vividly described American deep South. Shabby, post-war England receded, that brilliant world of balls became her world, *she* was Scarlett, wilful, spoilt, admired. Totally in the grip of this imagined landscape, Marianne was unaware of time passing until the book was suddenly wrenched from her hands. Only it wasn't Ashley Wilkes's sensitive face she was gazing at, but Gerald's slightly grubby one.

Still half in this other world, Marianne blinked. 'What the devil do you think you're up to?' she demanded.

'You've no right to be reading this.'

'Why ever not?'

'Because it was my mother's book and you are a servant.'

All Marianne's good intentions fled and she rose and advanced on him.

'Give me the book back.'

Gerald stared at her defiantly. 'Shan't,' he answered and stuffed the book up the front of his pullover.

Marianne shrugged. 'OK, keep it, but you can forget tonight.' She sat down, picked up a day-old *The Times* newspaper and began searching through the situations vacant columns.

Gerald pushed down the newspaper with the flat of his hand. 'But you promised!'

Marianne shook him off as if he were an irritating fly. 'No I didn't. Your father asked me. And might I remind you that it's my afternoon off and I was planning to go to the pictures in Leicester. But I give as good as I get and you can take a running jump.'

Gerald pulled the book from underneath his jumper and

placed it on her lap. 'You may read it if you like, Armstrong. And I'm very, very sorry.'

'Too late.' Marianne didn't look up from the situations vacant column.

'Please. I'll buy you a toffee apple.'

'Generous of you, I'm sure.' Marianne struggled to suppress a smile.

'Can we go then?'

Here is a motherless child, the voice of conscience reminded her. 'I suppose so. But I'm warning you, any more nonsense and your father will hear of it.'

'From now on I'll be good as gold, I promise.'

'Go and get some warm clothes on, then. I'll see you back down here in a quarter of an hour.'

Up in her room Marianne kissed the photograph of Nan, Renée and herself, taken on the front at Southend before the war. She was standing between them with a bucket and spade, and had a bow, like butterfly wings, in her hair. Renée was wearing beach pyjamas and Nan had on a linen dress and jacket. She could even remember the colour, daffodil-yellow to match her hair. But that was Nan for you, money burnt a hole in her pocket. If she had it she spent it, and they were always better turned out than anyone else in the street. And look at me now, reduced to wearing Renée's cast-offs. Pulling on a pair of khaki ATS trousers, she hitched them up with the strap from her suit-case. One of Miss Webb's homespun jumpers followed and last of all she stamped her feet into a pair of wellington boots she'd found in a cupboard. As she did so, Marianne wondered whether they had belonged to Felicity. If so they had the same size five feet, which she felt gave them a connection. On her way out, Marianne grabbed her coat from the door-hook. As she buttoned it up she heard that ghostly voice in her ear. 'God almighty, you look like a bleedin' refugee, luv.'

'Yeah, but a warm one, Nan,' Marianne retorted and shut the door on her interfering grandmother.

Gerald was sitting at the bottom of the stairs, thumb in mouth and rocking backwards and forwards. Without breaking her stride, Marianne called, 'Right, let's get going.'

'I've got to take Annie, where is she?'

Marianne pretended ignorance. 'Annie? Who's Annie?'

'My doll.'

'Sorry, no idea,' Marianne lied, for in fact she'd banished the repulsive creature to the cellar. 'What do you want it for, anyway?'

'To throw on the bonfire.'

'But there's already one there.'

'It doesn't make any difference. It's the custom in this family.'

'Not this year it isn't; now let's get going.'

'Not until I've found Annie.'

'Suit yourself.' Marianne jumped on her bicycle and started to pedal off.

'Hey, wait for me,' Gerald yelled.

Marianne, knowing it was no way for a grown woman to behave, slowed down. 'We'll hear no more about the doll, is that clear?'

Gerald nodded.

'Up you get then.' She held out her hand and hauled him on to the saddle. 'Now hold tight,' she ordered and set off down Fosse Lane. The night air was still, brilliant stars punctured the inky blackness of the sky and gazing upwards Marianne whispered, 'Hello Nan.'

'Who you talking to?'

'My grandmother. See that star twinkling extra bright? Well that's her.'

'That's rubbish. We go to heaven.'

'I ask you, where would God find the room for us all? No,

when we die our souls become stars. And my Nan was a real star. She should have been on the stage. And could she sing.' Particularly after a glass or two of stout, Marianne remembered. 'There wasn't a music-hall song she didn't know by heart. In fact the Camberwell Palace was her second home. Yeah, those were good old days, before Adolf went and spoilt it all.'

'I'm singing in the choir on Christmas Eve,' Gerald offered.

'Are you now?' Marianne answered, but without much interest, for they'd reached Stretton Magna. Slowing down, she stared. This couldn't be the silent village she'd arrived at a few days previously. Light poured from the public house, children zigzagged amongst the crowds waving sparklers, Morris men leapt up and down and the whole atmosphere struck Marianne as manic.

Gerald, obviously not wanting to be seen in the company of a servant, jumped from the saddle. Calling over his shoulder, 'There's Vealy,' he shot off across the Green in pursuit of another small boy.

Leaning the bike against a tree, Marianne thought: so Gerald's chummy with the butcher's son; that won't go down well with his father. Personally she was glad to know that he had at least one friend. It wasn't natural the way he lived, alone in that ghost-ridden house with only his weird grandmother for company. Marianne looked about her. Gerald was probably the only child here without his parents, and now she was planning to abandon him too. Marianne stifled a twinge of guilt. Gerald wasn't her business. If she stayed here, she'd end up as crazy as the rest of them.

'I'm going to get you a toffee apple like I promised, Armstrong,' the subject of her thoughts called as he and Vealy galloped past.

'I'll be over by the bonfire,' Marianne shouted back, noticing that many of the villagers nursed straw effigies. Again she had the impression of a world slightly out of kilter. She was also conscious of being an outsider in a close-knit society, so when she saw a face she recognized, she bounced over to him. 'Hello, Mr Veal,' she called a fraction too brightly.

The butcher, who was roping off the bonfire, looked up. 'Hello, m'dook.' But then some youngsters ducked under the barrier and he turned to deal with them. 'Clear off. Do you want to get yerselves cooked to a frazzle, like her up there?' he demanded and gave one fleeing child a clip round the ear.

'Kids, what can you say, no sense.' He peered at her closely. 'Now where do I know you from?'

'I've been into your shop. I work at Hope Grange.'

'Of course. I remember now.'

'Has Mr Lacey settled with you yet?'

'Came in this afternoon. Most apologetic he was.' The butcher began binding sticks with rag and dipping them into paraffin. 'We're bang up to date now, which makes a change. Gentry have funny notions about theirselves. They somehow think we should be grateful for their custom. Payment somehow don't come into it. But the war 'as changed things. The Laceys and their kind 'ave had their day, the future belongs to the likes of you and me.'

Marianne would like to have seen some sign of it, but she wasn't going to disagree with the purveyor of the best sausages and pork pies in Leicestershire. At least that's what those framed certificates that hung in his shop window claimed.

'I like to know all my customers by name, so what's yours, m'dook? asked Mr Veal.

'Marianne Armstrong.'

'Well, maid Marianne, what's yer opinion of the Laceys? I bet they're slave-drivers.'

Marianne shrugged noncommittally. This was a small village, tongues no doubt wagged and she still hadn't been paid.

'I can understand you not wantin' to say anything, but that

family have been throwing their weight around for centuries. And I don't suppose you need me to tell you that they're on their uppers and the house is falling down around their ears. I reckon Mr Hugo will be looking to sell it off soon. And a good job too. I'm on the parish council, and we're in dire need of decent housing in the village. I reckon there'd be room for twenty or more council houses on that land.'

'Oh, people wouldn't want to live there. The place is full of ghosts.' Appalled at letting her tongue run away with her, Marianne clapped her hand over her mouth. What was she saying? The butcher would think she was crazy. But luckily a man called, 'Come on, let's get this bonfire going, Alf,' and Mr Veal moved away. They lit the torches, then set off in opposite directions, thrusting them into the base of the bonfire as they went. The wood was damp and it took a while for it to get going, but then, with a whoosh, flames shot into the air. A great cheer went up, then villagers came running and began hurling the straw effigies on to the fire. Then to the solemn beating of a single drum they linked hands and, chanting in some strange tongue, they began a slow, ritualistic dance round the fire.

The heat was so intense that Marianne was forced to step back. As she watched their faces became misshapen and ugly, like the church gargoyles. It was a scene so primitive that Marianne felt the hairs rise on the back of her neck. A moment ago they were ordinary folk, a little the worse for drink, now they were behaving like savages.

Guessing the reason, Marianne glanced upwards. The doll was still there, her red shoes protruding from her skirt, and awaiting her fate. The golden ball of fire shifted and in its glow the creature seemed to be pleading with her. Marianne had an eerie sense of some connection between them. Dizzy and confused, certain she could smell burning flesh, Marianne turned away. 'Burn the witch! Burn the witch! Burn the witch!' the crowd began to chant, and through the wavering heat Marianne caught a glimpse of Hugo Lacey. Simultaneously on a light breeze, she heard the faint jingle of bells; then, of their own accord, tears began to course slowly down her cheeks.

Chapter Three

'Armstrong, *whom* do you know in America?' Gerald demanded, waving a letter in the air.

'None of your business and give it here.' The boy's condescending tone irritated her and Marianne snatched the envelope from him.

'Will you save the stamp for me?' Now that he was after something, Gerald's tone was more conciliatory.

'Maybe. Now off you go to school.'

'Aren't you going to open your letter?'

'In a moment.'

Reluctantly Gerald went and Marianne slit open the envelope. She'd sent Renée her new address before leaving London, but in her more despondent moments, and there were plenty of these, she feared that with such vast distances separating them, the frail family links would be permanently severed. Her aunt hadn't said so, but Marianne also got the impression that life was far too hectic for her to be spending it writing letters. Usually those that did come through the door were addressed to her employer, either official things with OHMS stamped on the envelope or from his bank.

But bless her, in the end, Renée had come up trumps. As Marianne unfolded the flimsy airmail paper it gave off a faint whiff of her aunt's favourite perfume and to bridge the miles, she sat with it pressed against her cheek while remembering the past, and struggling to hold back the tears.

Dear Mary, oops sorry, Marianne,

I hope you're sitting down because I think you're going to get a shock when you hear my news. I'm coming home! I didn't let on in my last letter, but things haven't worked out as I hoped they would for Chuck and me – to tell the truth, he's a heavy drinker and after a couple of black eyes and a split lip I thought to myself, you don't have to put up with this Renée old girl, and did a runner. Pittsburgh stinks so I came to New York to try and get some money together. Anyway, what I want to say is, stay where you are or we might never find each other again. You're all the family I've got and from now on you and me will stick together like glue. Men are selfish buggers and I regret ever marrying, but we all make mistakes, and I'm going to put it down to experience and move on.

I'll try and let you know when I'm leaving and I'm really excited at the thought of seeing you again. If I can afford it I'll buy us both some pretty dresses and we'll be the snazziest girls in all England. You never saw such a waste of food as there is in the restaurant where I worked; gallons of milk poured down the drain, loaves chucked in the trash-can. Knowing all about rationing and going without, I get really steamed up about it and I told a customer off for leaving most of his dinner on the plate. I said didn't he know people were starving in Europe. Of course he reported me and I've been sacked. When will I learn to keep my big mouth shut?

Anyway there's plenty of work and as soon as I've got something I'll send my address. I never thought I'd miss shabby old England, but I do, and I miss you even more, sweetheart, but we'll be together soon, I promise. Hope you like your new job, although it sounds a bit in the wilds. But remember, I love you. So long toots, love and kisses, Renée.

Her aunt was coming home. Marianne blew here nose and wiped her eyes. Well, she says she is, because there was no getting away from it, Renée was a bit of a one for the blokes. If she met another one, in the first flush of love she and dear old England would be forgotten. And even if that didn't happen, it could be months before she got a berth on a ship. Until Renée's letter arrived she couldn't wait to be gone from this weird household. Now she had no choice but to stay and run around after that old battle-axe, she muttered in response to the impatient ringing of Mrs Lacey's bell.

The old woman was sitting up in bed, still tugging at the bell-cord when Marianne walked in with her breakfast.

'About time. Are you trying to starve me to death?'

Marianne laid the tray across the bed. 'Don't put ideas into my head,' she muttered as she went and drew back the curtains.

'What was that?'

'I said it's a nice morning. Quite sunny.'

'And this is quite inedible.' Mrs Lacey threw down the toast, tasted her tea and made a face. 'And this is cold.' Since this was an almost daily ritual, Marianne picked up the tray without comment and stood awaiting her orders.

'I want you to polish the stairs and balusters today. After that go and see if that frightful butcher has any mince. And not all fat, either, tell him.'

'It's cash on the nail or nothing. Those were Mr Veal's words.'

'I know, I know.'

Marianne studied Mrs Lacey, the aggrieved slope of her shoulders, the sour expression, and wondered about her past. It would have been a privileged upbringing, but the world that she assumed would always provide for her every whim had been ironed flat by war, which probably accounted for her permanent state of irritability.

'Well, go and get on with that polishing. You're not paid to stand around.'

'I'm not paid full stop.'

'What?'

'I said I haven't been paid yet.'

'My son will deal your wages.'

'You said that last week, madam,' Marianne reminded her employer and went to find the polish and dusters. Like everything else at Hope Grange, the balusters were ingrained with dirt. Even Mrs Lacey, Marianne reflected, as she gouged the muck from the elaborate carvings, would benefit from a good scrub with Vim. But with a bit of elbow grease the staircase polished up a treat and she kept herself cheerful thinking about Renée and the prospect of having her home soon.

Marianne was massaging her knees when the rattle of a stick along the balusters called her to attention. Above her stood Mrs Lacey. She was wearing a pair of white gloves and Marianne's immediate thought was that she'd decided to go to the butcher's herself, although the only occasion she'd seen her venture outside was to the church last Sunday.

But then, without a word, she began to descend the stairs, pausing to run her gloved hands down each baluster. Marianne watched her with a perplexed frown. What an earth was she up to? Mrs Lacey reached the bottom of the stairs and swung round with palms upturned like Al Jolson. 'Dust!' she trumpeted.

Marianne stared at the gloves. They were a virgin white. She'd had enough. From now on it was open warfare.

'Them balusters haven't been touched since the year dot and you know it, so if they're not to your liking, do them yourself.' She flung the duster at Mrs Lacey's feet and strode past her, so consumed with rage she could barely breathe. In her room

Marianne rushed to the window, flung it open and sucked in the frosty air. That woman really had gone too far, and she was going to speak to Captain Lacey. He wouldn't like a servant criticizing his mother, but she had one advantage over Mrs Lacey; she could cook.

Having calculated that she could win this battle, Marianne calmed down. She was about to close the window when she noticed a pheasant in the garden below. He'd make a tasty meal she thought. But the bird's bright plumage had drawn her eyes to something else, footmarks on the frozen grass. Apart from the postman, few people came up to the house and Mrs Lacey never went in to the garden. The thought of someone out there, probably up to no good, made Marianne's flesh creep, and she remembered the tramp she'd bought the rabbit from. From there her mind leapt to the chickens. Well, he wouldn't get his thieving mitts on those.

Taking the stairs two at a time, Marianne grabbed a hockey stick from the hall-stand and went charging outside. The sun didn't reach the back of the house at this time of the year, so it was easy to follow the footprints, and in the silence Marianne heard the sound of a spade hacking at the frozen earth. She paused. Could it be another ghostly visitation? Immediately she dismissed the idea as fanciful. She didn't believe in the supernatural and what she'd seen the other day had been a trick of the light.

At least ghosts were benign, but Marianne's bravery didn't extend to becoming the victim of a poacher's gun, so she approached her quarry with extreme caution, hockey stick held high and ready to strike. And then she saw him, hard at work *stealing* her vegetables.

We'll soon see about that! Incensed, Marianne stepped out from behind the bush. 'Stop! At once!' she ordered. The man swung round, saw he was within a quarter of an inch of having his skull cracked open and leapt out of the way. As he did his foot tangled with the spade and a second later he was lying on the ground.

'And what do you think you're up to?' Marianne demanded, as he heaved himself to his feet.

'*Bitte?*'

'What are you doing here?' she repeated.

'I am, how do you say, digging garden.'

'Stealing more like it.'

'I do not steal, I work for captain,' the young man replied with dignity. Simultaneously Marianne took in the heavily accented English and the dark brown uniform and began to sweat. Bloody hell, a German prisoner of war. A poacher was nothing in comparison.

Look him straight in the eye and show him you're not frightened, Marianne told herself and, struggling to sound normal, she asked, 'So who gave you permission to come here?'

'The camp commandant. Captain Lacey asked for a good person to help with garden and I was chosen.' It was clear he considered this a privilege.

Marianne's grip loosened on the hockey stick. Cheap labour like me, not some criminal.

'Did the captain not tell you this? You are his wife, yes?'

'Oh … no.' Marianne glanced down at her floral, wrap-around apron and stifled a giggle. Felicity in this dowdy garment? Never. 'I just work here. Not that it's any of your business, and I shouldn't be talking to you either,' she added, remembering who and what he was.

'Why is that?'

'Because we are enemies.'

'Not any longer. And who will hear us, see us? No one but the birds, I think, and they will not tell anybody.'

'That's beside the point. I'm far too busy to stand around

gossiping, and you've got plenty to do so you'd better get on with it.' As Marianne began to walk away the young man called after her, 'I am cold and I am thirsty. Will you not bring me a drink?'

'No.'

But later, as she spooned tea into the pot and filled it with boiling water, she remembered how inadequate his uniform had looked. And there's plenty of tea in the pot, for heaven's sake, she told herself and filled a lemonade bottle. As she wrapped a cloth round it she could hear, above her, Mrs Lacey's wireless. *Workers' Playtime*: it was one of the old lady's favourite programmes. With luck she wouldn't stir until it was finished. But fraternizing with POWs was against the law, and it would give Mrs Lacey great pleasure to report her to the authorities; no German was worth being prosecuted for.

By the time Marianne reached the vegetable patch her charitable instincts had all but drained away and she thrust the bottle at the surprised young German in a resentful manner. 'There you are.'

'You are a very kind English lady, thank you.' He gave a slight bow and swigged back the tea in great thirsty gulps.

'You needn't think I'm going to make a habit of it.'

He paused and wiped his mouth with the back of his hand. 'Oh.'

'Tea, sugar, milk are all rationed you know,' Marianne reminded him testily.

'Yes. I am sorry. Water will do in future. But will you tell me your name, Fräulein?'

'No.'

'Well, I will tell you mine.'

'Don't bother; I'm not interested,' Marianne retorted, and hurried away.

However when Gerald arrived home from school she tackled him about the POW.

'Did you know your father has taken on a German to work in

the garden?' She spread plum jam on to a slice of bread and handed it to him.

Gerald took a large bite then wiped his hand across his jam-smeared mouth. 'But Father hates the Hun.'

Not when it comes to cheap labour, Marianne thought cynically. Aloud she said, 'So do I for killing my Nan and flattening London.'

Gerald aimed an imaginary gun at her. 'Shall l go and shoot him dead for you?'

'That won't be necessary, thank you.'

'Daddy killed a hundred on D Day.'

'He had time to stop and count them, did he?'

Gerald shrugged away this question, stuffed the rest of the bread in to his mouth, and raced to the door. 'I'm going out to have a look at him.'

'He's not a prize exhibit in the circus,' Marianne called after him. But Gerald had already gone and didn't return until it was almost dark.

'Franz has gone back to camp,' he announced as he walked through the door. 'The lorry came to pick him up. They live in Nissen huts out by the railway line.'

'So who gave you permission to call him by his first name?'

'He did.'

'Children don't call adults by their first names, it's not proper.'

'He's only a prisoner of war.'

'It makes no difference.'

'His other name is Hartmann.'

'I don't want to hear another word about him, is that clear?'

Gerald lifted his shoulders, then let them drop. 'Oh, all right.'

'And if I catch you fraternizing again I'll inform your father.'

'Yes, Armstrong.' He gave a weary sigh.

'Now go and wash your hands and comb your hair, you look as if you've been dragged through a hedge backwards.'

In spite of her threats to Gerald, as she went about her work in the gloomy house, Marianne often found herself pausing at upstairs windows. To check that the POW was getting on with his work was the excuse she made, while trying to assess his age: twenty-four at a guess. And looks? Well, no Clark Gable but passable. His hair was light brown and thick and straight, and he didn't have much meat on his bones, but who did these days, Marianne reflected. Occasionally he would stop and lean on his spade, but he was no slacker and gradually and methodically the vegetable plot and flower-beds were tidied up, trees pruned and branches sawn into logs and left outside the kitchen door, always neatly stacked.

Marianne was growing so desperate for the company of someone of her own age that she was frequently tempted to invite him into the kitchen. It was when she found herself thinking of him as Franz that she knew she needed to be on her guard. Her prejudices were in danger of dissolving, which wouldn't do at all.

Fortunately Saturday was approaching, with an afternoon off, plus two weeks' wages to dispose of. Marianne had worked out exactly how she would spend her few hours of freedom. After catching the bus into Leicester she would wander round Joseph Johnson's admiring the fashions, then treat herself to afternoon tea at the Turkey Café, where Miss Webb had once taken her on her birthday. After this she would see what was showing at the cinema.

However, on the Saturday, one, two, three, four o'clock came and went with no sign of Hugo Lacey or her wages. At five o'clock he breezed into the kitchen and slapped three one-pound notes on to the table. 'There you are, Armstrong, your wages. A bit late but I don't imagine there's much to spend it on in this damnable village.'

'I was planning to go into Leicester.'

Hugo Lacey glanced at the clock. 'Well, you still have time, there's a bus at 5.30,' he replied, then turned and strode out of the kitchen.

'Thanks for your concern, Mr Lacey,' she shot back, but he'd gone, after spending all of five minutes in the house. And Gerald was staying at a friend's house for the night, so she wouldn't even have the dubious pleasure of his company.

Well, she had no intention of spending the evening staring at four walls. She'd seen a poster in the butchers so she knew there was a dance in the village hall tonight and she would go to that. At least there'd be music, and people of her own age, and someone might even ask her to dance.

She put two flat irons to heat on the hob; when they had warmed up she ironed her best blue-rayon dress, polished her red shoes, then ran a bath. Although the water looked a bit rusty it was hot so, indulging herself, Marianne filled the bath almost to the rim, then relaxed into it with a sigh of contentment. After giving herself a good soaping she washed her hair, dried herself on a miserable piece of towelling and scuttled back to her freezing bedroom. Here she dressed, carefully rolling on the precious nylons that Renée had sent her. They were like gossamer and some clumsy-footed young man was bound to ladder them, but they'd been sent to be worn and she had legs worth showing off. And why not slap on the war paint while she was at it? Go the whole hog. 'No point in hiding your light under a bushel,' – how often had she heard her aunt say that? Well, tonight she would make sure she shone, like a star.

Marianne opened her compact, dabbed powder on her nose, then outlined her mouth with lipstick, a bold red to match her shoes. 'Hussy,' she accused her reflection, laughed and pulled a brush through her still damp curls. Although she couldn't see much of herself, she reckoned she'd get a dance or two tonight, and after checking that her seams were straight and she had money, comb and lipstick, Marianne opened her bedroom door.

Someone was singing 'Red Sails in the Sunset' on Mrs Lacey's wireless and Marianne floated down the stairs in time to the music. With a jivey kick she pushed open the kitchen door and stared in disbelief. A pile of snow lay dissolving on the floor, while the back door creaked back and forth on rusty hinges. Marianne hurried over and peered out into the night. The snow was falling thick and silent as goose feathers at Christmas, drifts were already forming around the house and there wasn't a cat's chance in hell of getting to the dance.

Marianne slammed the door and stared miserably at the expanding pool of water. It could stay there. And after all the effort of getting ready! She gave a sob of self pity and looked at the clock. Still only seven o'clock. She paced up and down chewing on her knuckles and looked again. One minute past seven. Never had time passed so slowly. Feeling cast adrift from the rest of the world, Marianne picked up, *Gone With The Wind*. But tonight she was unable to make that imaginative leap from a snowbound northern country to the heat of Atlanta and she flicked the pages back and forth in an aimless sort of way. As she did, Marianne became aware of something between the pages. Holding the book by its covers, she shook it. A piece of paper fluttered to the ground. As she bent to pick it up she saw that it was a letter, or rather part of a letter, because it had been torn up then stuck together again, and bits of it were missing. But the recipient's name was still intact and Marianne started to read the letter with a guilty rush of excitement.

My dearest, beloved, most precious Felicity,
I beg of you, please see me tonight. I will wait for you in the stables. They are transferring me to another bomber station, obviously I can't say where, so it will be our last chance to be

together. I'm so desperate and sick with love for you I swear I will desert if I have to leave without holding your lovely body in my arms one las ...

The love letter ended there, and the signature was missing, but the man's passion for her employer's wife leapt off the page and it didn't take much to guess what they'd got up to in the stables. During the war, too, when Hugo Lacey was away serving his country. Their deceit burnt Marianne's fingers and the letter fluttered from her fingers. And there was she assuming Felicity was dead, when more likely she'd run off with her lover. Dissatisfaction must have driven her into another man's arms, and yet the inscription in the book showed Hugo to be a loving husband. Losing his wife like that must have pole-axed him and no doubt some of the locals had enjoyed seeing a man of such monumental pride brought low.

Although Marianne realized that she'd stumbled on something tragic, part of her envied Felicity. No one would ever love her with such intensity, she was far too ordinary. She picked up the letter again, and was studying it for a clue that might reveal mysterious airman's identity, when the back door flew open and a driving, icy wind rushed in and plucked the letter from her hand. 'Dratted door,' Marianne muttered as she pursued the letter across the kitchen, grabbed it and at the same time collided with Hugo Lacey as he stepped across the threshold. Her heart almost stopped beating, but she stuttered, a 'sorry,' backed away from him and managed to slip the letter between the pages of the book. She glanced at her employer to see if he'd noticed and quailed, for his expression was thunderous.

'The bloody car broke down. I've had to walk miles.' He pushed his foot against the door to close it, but it swung open again. 'Close, you bugger!' This time he kicked the wooden panel with such ferocity that Marianne expected his foot to go through it.

This was not the time of year to be without a door, so with an, 'Excuse me, sir,' Marianne brushed past him and pressed her shoulder against it until the latch clicked. She then turned the key and bolted it. 'The wood is warped, it needs planing down.' Her tone made it clear that this was a job well within his capabilities.

'Get that Hun to deal with it.' He removed his greatcoat and cap, shook off the snow, and threw them on the chair.

Marianne was an expert on drunks for Nan had often been legless on a Saturday night and she could see that her employer was well and truly plastered. But drunks came in all varieties; happy, sad, self-pitying or, worst of all, fighting drunk. Clearly Hugo Lacey belonged to this last group; the charm had been superficial and he was just a common drunk now.

He made his way to the fire as if walking a tightrope and held his hands to the flames.

'Am I glad to see this.'

'The fire's laid in the sitting room, sir, you only have to put a match to it.' Marianne wanted company but not this.

'I prefer it here.' He turned and studied her. 'If I may say so, you look extremely becoming, Miss Marianne Armstrong. Lots of bright lipstick.'

Marianne shifted uncomfortably.

'It must be for some young man.'

'No, just a dance at the village hall.'

'And the snow stopped you. What a pity, although I hope you weren't intending to wear those shoes.'

'Well, it was these or a pair of wellington boots,' Marianne retorted.

'Don't you realize that no decent woman in these parts would be seen in red shoes? Take them off.' Hugo Lacey bore down on her, but Marianne faced him squarely. Just let him touch me and he'll feel it where it hurts. But his glance had gone past her to the book lying on the table and he picked it up.

Her face stiff with anxiety, Marianne waited. This was it. But Hugo Lacey had opened the book at the flyleaf and as he read his own loving dedication to Felicity, his face darkened. 'Like this sort of tripe, do you?' He threw the book back on the table.

'Yes.'

'You women are all the same, and all you think about is romance.' His voice was hard-edged, holding a hint of violence. Uneasily aware of how isolated she was, Marianne stepped behind the table. But he stared round the kitchen as if searching for something; then he picked up his coat and cap and left.

'Goodbye and good riddance,' she muttered and felt the tension ebb from her body. In need of refreshment she put the kettle on. She was about to make the tea, when, to her dismay, Hugo Lacey returned, this time carrying a wind-up gramophone, some records and a bottle of whisky, all of which he dumped on the table.

'You don't want tea. A drop of the hard stuff will do you far more good. Here.' He poured a good measure of whisky into Marianne's cup, took a swig from the bottle, then began to wind up the gramophone. 'I have decided that you look so charming, it would be a shame if you were deprived of your evening of fun. If you can't go to the dance, then you shall have it here.' He sorted through the records, found what he wanted, dropped it on the turntable and the grim, cavernous kitchen filled with the sound of a woman's voice, singing sweetly and poignantly, *All Shadows Fly Away*.

'May I?' Hugo Lacey asked formally, and it was all so surreal that Marianne allowed him to take her hand. She found herself pressed hard against his brass buttons. With a sober partner she danced well, but Hugo Lacey was so far gone he didn't know his left foot from his right and they stumbled around the kitchen, with all the grace of a couple of baby elephants. In this enforced intimacy, she was acutely aware of his hand pressed into the small of her back, and she found herself thinking: once in some grand ballroom, he would have held Felicity, his wife, the woman he loved, in his arms like this. And now here he is dancing with a domestic in a cheerless kitchen. What a come-down. When he started to croon in her ear, Marianne was so struck by the absurdity of the situation she stifled a nervous giggle and wondered whether it was possible to die of embarrassment. He got as far as, 'the day you left, the day you went from me ...', then his voice faltered and he made a strange choking sound. Marianne glanced up. Were those tears? She felt a moment of pity for him, but then, with a great roar, he flung her aside, snatched up the record and broke it across his knee.

'We'll have no more of that stupid song.' He glared at Marianne, glugged down the rest of the whisky, tucked the bottle under his arm, and staggered from the room.

Maybe if I stand stock-still I will stop shaking, Marianne said to herself. She'd always thought she understood the mind of a drunk, but this really was the weirdest evening of her life. Hard to imagine now that, earlier, she'd longed for company.

Outside in the hall Hugo Lacey was giving a good impression of a man going berserk. Marianne heard wood splintering, vases and ornaments smashing to the floor, all in a frustrated search for booze, she suspected. She pressed her hands over her ears. Where was the old lady? Why didn't she deal with her drunken son?

The smashing and cursing continued for a good ten minutes, then it went quiet. Guessing he'd run out of ammunition, Marianne waited for him to move on to the many unused rooms. But a strange, brooding silence had descended, which was almost as unnerving as his ranting. If only she could get to her bedroom. She tiptoed to the door and peered through the keyhole. The hall was as ill lit as the rest of the house, and she could just make out an upturned chair. She eased open the door and found herself in a combat zone. Picking her way through the debris, Marianne righted a couple of chairs, resisted the urge to get a broom and sweep up the mess, continued in a straight course towards the stairs, and almost went flying over the prostate body of Hugo Lacey.

Marianne stared down at him. Rich man, poor man, drink was a great leveller especially when you're lying flat out on the floor. He'd subjected her to one of the weirdest, most frightening experiences in her life, and her instinct was to leave him to get on with it. However, it was freezing in the hall and she could do without his death on her conscience. She reached for his army greatcoat hanging on the newel post, threw it over him, then placed a cushion under his head. 'Dead to the world and all its sorrows,' she mused. As she spoke he moved restlessly, flinging his arm wide and dislodging the coat. She bent to cover him again, tucking it in this time. He mumbled a few words, and Marianne caught the name Felicity. Knowing he would have to face his own demons in the morning, she experienced again an unwelcome feeling of pity.

Chapter Four

Marianne threw out an arm to silence the alarm clock, saw her breath condense as it hit the frigid air and, simultaneously, at the edge of her mind, she had a recollection of something unpleasant, like a leftover nightmare. Reluctant to deal with it she slid back under the bedclothes. She was dozing off when, downstairs, a door slammed. Instantly she was awake and clear-brained. She leapt out of bed and raced barefoot down the short stairway to the landing window. However, she was too late; the only evidence of Hugo Lacey's flight from his demons were his footprints already filling with snow. Teeth chattering, Marianne scampered back to her room. At least she was saved from the embarrassment of having to face him in the unforgiving light of a Sunday morning, although she supposed there would be some tidying up to do.

Well, there was no point in delaying it. Marianne poked at the disc of ice in the washstand jug, splashed a few drops of freezing water on to her face, dried it and dressed. 'As if I don't have enough to do without clearing up after a drunk,' she complained, and hitched her stockings to her suspenders with a resentful tug. And where had his mother been last night? She must have heard the commotion. But Mrs Lacey was afflicted with various unspecified ailments, the main one being idleness in Marianne's opinion, and this prevented her from doing anything more exacting than the daily crossword.

But then the whole family is useless, Marianne reflected. She started off downstairs, reached the hall and stared in disbelief. 'Blimey, what's happened here?' she exclaimed, for every last piece of porcelain had been swept away, presumably by the guilty party. If it hadn't been for the gramophone still sitting on the kitchen table she might have begun to wonder if she dreamed the whole weird incident.

Drunks and remorse went together like ham and eggs and he must have been feeling it by the bucket-load when he woke with a fat head and stiff limbs and found himself eye-level with the wreckage, all of his own doing.

'Well let's hope that's the last we've seen of him for a while,' Marianne muttered. To celebrate she wound up the gramophone, dropped a record on the turntable and began to dance around the room in time to Glenn Miller and his orchestra. Immediately her mood lightened and she made up the fire, prepared some porridge and drizzled golden syrup over it, all to the tune of *String Of Pearls*. As the solid warmth of the porridge spread through her, so did a sense of her own worth. This lot really depend on me, she decided.

Nevertheless, when she took the old lady a plate of porridge Marianne was ready for the usual string of complaints. Amazingly Mrs Lacey picked up her spoon and started to eat without a word, and it occurred to Marianne that it might have been she who had come down and cleared up her drunken son's mess. It was out of character, because she was idle by nature, but family honour was at stake. As they did from time to time, unwanted feelings of pity for the woman welled up in her. What a sad empty life. All she had was her pride and a sense of superiority. No friends or neighbours visited and, apart from church, she appeared to have no social life. Meanwhile her son, her pride and joy was sinking into a alcoholic haze, and had been so drunk last night he'd danced with his domestic, even told her she was beautiful. Marianne stifled a giggle, and Mrs Lacey paused, spoon halfway to her mouth.

'Did you say something?'

'No madam.' Marianne could detect a wariness in Mrs Lacey's tone as it suddenly clicked that the servant standing in front of her knew every damn thing that had gone on the previous night, and she could spread gossip about it around the village.

With some difficulty Mrs Lacey formed her mouth into a smile. 'A very enjoyable breakfast … thank you.'

Marianne nearly keeled over from shock, then she saw her employer fumble in her purse and draw out at ten-shilling note. Pressing it into Marianne's hand, she said, 'Treat yourself to something nice.'

Marianne wasn't sure what to do. She still hadn't been paid all her wages, but it offended her that Mrs Lacey trusted her so little that she assumed that for ten bob she would keep her mouth shut. She handed the money back. 'Thank you, madam, but it is not necessary to bribe me.' With that she picked up the tray and left the room.

Not long after this, Gerald returned from his night with his friend and Marianne gave him the Sunday paper to take up to his grandmother. He didn't spend long with her and after a cup of hot milk he announced that he was going outside to make a snowman for Franz. But a thaw had set in and he came in to tell her he was off to church. He was in the choir, and had to practise for the Christmas Eve service, he explained.

The next morning, when the POW lorry drove past the kitchen window, Gerald grabbed his satchel and ran. 'Got to go, Fred the driver said he'd give me a lift to school.'

'But it's probably not allowed. And what will your father say?' Marianne protested. However it was to deaf ears and through the window she saw the tail-board let down, Franz jump out and outstretched arms haul Gerald in. Then as the aged lorry with its disintegrating exhaust pipe phut-phutted down the drive the back door swung open. Remembering Hugo Lacey's instructions to get it fixed, Marianne ran out to the yard. 'Excuse me, er uhm' she called, not sure how she should address the young German.

Franz, who was halfway down the path, turned. 'You are speaking to me, Fräulein?'

'Yes. Captain Lacey wants you to fix the kitchen door. It's warped.'

'Warped?'

'The wood is swollen because of the snow and it's difficult to close.'

'Ah yes. You have something I could use to make it better?'

'You'll need a plane.'

Franz's face was a study. 'An aeroplane?'

Marianne giggled. 'No, it's a thing for shaving off wood. Wait while I get my coat. There's all sorts of junk in the stables, we'll probably find one there.'

As soon as she stepped through the stable door Marianne remembered the love-letter and blushed, for along with the smell of straw, leather and horses, there was an underlying odour of lust and adultery. And whispers, feminine whispers, sweet and persuasive, drawing her into that act of betrayal. It's nonsense, an over-active imagination, stop it! But there is was again.

'Can you hear that whispering?' she blurted out, then felt foolish when Franz gave her a puzzled look.

'There is only you and me, so who can be whispering?'

'The ghosts.'

The corner of his mouth tilted. 'I think it is just mouses in the hay.'

'I've seen them,' Marianne insisted, 'Right outside the stables, horses too, so please don't smirk.'

'I am sorry, Fräulein, for my smirk, but I was student before the

war, and my subjects were the sciences, and I am a rational
person, so I do not believe in the supernatural.' Then, obviously
deciding the matter was at an end, he began rummaging through
a toolbox.

Marianne gave him a hard look. Oh don't you, Mr Clever-
clogs? A bit of a superior attitude for one of the defeated, she
thought sniffily. But why should I care what a thin, shabby
nobody whose opinions count for nothing, thinks, anyway? And
showing off like that with a few long words isn't going to impress
me. Well, she wasn't going to waste time explaining, but she'd
always been sensitive to atmosphere, a great gift according to her
grandmother. But she mustn't let it get personal. After all, their
sole reason for being here was to find a tool that would sort out
the door problem. Marianne looked about her. If only she knew
where to start, for it was clear that the Laceys rarely threw
anything away.

Cobwebs clung to decades of junk: toys some child must have
treasured, garden tools, furniture, ancient perambulators and
boxes of heaven knows what. More interesting was a well-trav-
elled trunk covered with the labels of about every country and
shipping line on the planet. Marianne lifted the lid. It was stuffed
full of evening gowns and she plunged her hands down amongst
the froth of silk, chiffon and georgette in greedy delight. Felicity
was almost a physical presence now and, pulling out a slim-fitting
oyster-satin evening dress with a label that said: *designed by
Schiaparelli*, Marianne held it against her. 'How do I look?' she
asked and did a little pirouette.

Franz studied her at some length, then replied, 'Beautiful.'

Feeling her cheeks redden, Marianne bent and stuffed the dress
back in the trunk. He was a foreigner, and they were given to flattery, and she must not allow herself be carried away by it. She
was not beautiful and never would be.

'Show me another dress,' Franz coaxed.

'No.' Marianne dropped the lid and his face fell.

'The dresses, who do they belong to?' he asked.

'Mr Lacey's wife, I suppose.'

'She does not live in the house, I think.'

'Maybe Captain Lacey keeps her locked up in the attic.'

Franz looked alarmed. 'But she would die up there.'

'Only joking,' Marianne smiled, realizing that it wasn't only war and language that divided them but humour, too.

'You were – how do you say – pulling my leg?'

Marianne nodded. 'But we mustn't get distracted. It's Monday and I've loads to do. Washing, shopping, there's never an end to it.'

'I think I have found what we are looking for.' Franz waved a plane in front of her. 'So I can now go and make your door better.'

As Franz worked, shaving off the excess wood at a steady pace, Marianne, thought: he's going to be useful to have around the place. When he was sure the door opened and closed without jamming, he sanded down any rough edges.

'It is nice in here, warm,' he observed as he swept up the wood-shavings and put them on the fire.

Hint, hint, thought Marianne, unable to believe anyone could find anything positive to say about the dreary kitchen. But he had spared her a winter of chilblains, so he was entitled to some reward. 'Why don't you sit down while I make a cup of coffee?'

'Thank you.'

'Your English is good,' Marianne observed as she spooned Camp coffee into two mugs and added hot water and sugar.

'I was in America for three years before I came here to England.'

'How did you get to be there?'

Franz took a sip of his coffee before replying. 'I served as a wireless operator on a U-boat. It was sunk in the Atlantic. Only three of us survived. We clung to a piece of wood for two days.'

But Marianne didn't want her emotions engaged, to feel pity, and she tried not to think of clutching fingers turning white and the icy Atlantic waters closing over his companions' heads.

Franz was staring into his coffee cup and obviously trying to control his emotions, but after a moment he cleared his throat and looked up. 'We were rescued by an American warship, then sent to Mississippi to pick cotton.'

'What was that like?'

'Hard, but better than being on a U-boat. And the Americans, they give us good food. When the war ended, they put us on a ship and took us to Belgium. The Belgians, they spat at us, but we were so happy because we thought we were going back to our homeland. Instead they sent us over here, to England.' His face had grown pale, his expression withdrawn.

'And you are unhappy?'

He gave her a wan smile. 'Yes, because my home, which is in Berlin, is now in the Russian zone and I do not want to go there.'

A peremptory jangling of the bell told Marianne she was required upstairs. 'That's the old lady. More orders I expect.'

Franz stood up and clicked his heels. 'Thank you for the coffee, Fräulein.'

'And thank you for fixing the door. It will keep the draughts out.'

They each went their separate ways, he out into the cold, Marianne upstairs to get the shopping list to take to Miss Hardcastle's emporium for the weekly rations.

'Still at that place, are you, missy?' Miss Hardcastle enquired as Marianne handed over the ration books.

'Yes, I'm still there, Miss Hardcastle.' Marianne replied, and maybe it was in reward for endeavour, because the shopkeeper was now a fraction more pleasant and sometimes even a few of life's luxuries made their way over the counter. Today Marianne was offered a tin of pink salmon. Fish pie tonight, she decided, as the shopkeeper cut out the points.

Taking advantage of her unusually mellow mood, Marianne asked, 'You wouldn't by any chance have five Woodbines, Miss Hardcastle?'

'Smoke, do you?'

'Now and then.'

The shop-owner slapped a slim green packet on the counter. 'There you are: five coffin nails. She smoked as well, y'know.'

'Who did?'

'Her from the house.' Mrs Hardcastle sniffed. 'Along with everything else.'

Since she was so obviously alluding to Felicity, Marianne felt free to probe. 'Did Mrs Lacey go away?'

Miss Hardcastle tapped the side of her nose. 'Ask no questions, and you'll get told no lies. And that'll be five shillings if you don't mind. Next please,' this to a woman who had just walked in through the door.

Felicity was very much on Marianne's mind as she cycled home, so much so that as she walked through the graveyard she stopped to check the Lacey headstones and vaults. She wasn't expecting to find her name amongst the deceased and she was right. As she continued it occurred to Marianne that she was allowing Felicity to become something of an obsession. Often she found herself holding her cup as she imagined Felicity might have done. And Felicity would have had a tinkling laugh. She tried that until she started getting funny looks, and realized that, from loneliness, she was making a companion out of an illusion.

It would have to stop or she'd go crackers. The non-fraternization laws were also stupid and deserved to be broken, Marianne decided and as soon as she got home she slipped the packet of cigarettes into her pocket and went outside to share one with Franz.

As she approached the stables Marianne sniffed burning leaves. Franz was having a bonfire.

But the leaves were too wet to do much more than smoulder and Franz was sitting on an upturned box trying to poke some life into the fire. He was obviously deep in thought, because when Marianne touched him on the shoulder, he jumped.

'Did you think I was a ghost?' she teased.

'No I did not, Fräulein. I was thinking about the potatoes I am cooking in the fire. They will soon be ready. Would you like one?'

'Yes please.' Forgetting the drawing room she'd been told to clean out, Marianne sat down on a box and watched Franz prod about in the fire. Eventually a couple of charred objects rolled out on to the ground.

With a clean cloth Franz picked one up and pierced the skin with a penknife. Steam and an appetizing smell floated out. He handed the potato to Marianne. 'Be careful or you will burn your mouth.'

In spite of its unpromising appearance, the potato tasted delicious. When they'd finished Marianne produced the cigarettes and offered one to Franz. They were smoking in companionable silence when Marianne heard a faint sound and cocked her ear.

'Listen,' she said and clutched Franz's arm. Into the winter tranquillity came the clatter of hoofs and voices. 'It's them! The ghosts!'

Franz stared at Marianne, then leapt to his feet and ran to investigate.

'Well?' she said when he sat down again.

'Do not worry, it is only the hunt going by on the road.' He smiled and went back to smoking his Woodbine.

Chapter Five

As they moved into December and the festive season approached, Marianne found herself remembering, with great gusts of longing, Christmases with her Nan and Renée before the war. Although now, as an adult able to do her sums, it was a puzzle where the money had come from, as a child she'd taken for granted the bulging pillowcase hanging at the bottom of her bed on Christmas morning, the food, the drink. And the fun didn't end there because on Boxing Day practically the whole street, along with several crates of stout, would crowd into their front parlour for a sing-song round the piano and a bit of a knees-up. Marianne sighed; ah, the good old days. And what had she got to look forward to now? Damn all.

There certainly wouldn't be any singing in this dreary house and if past behaviour was anything to go by, Hugo Lacey would be well in his cups by the time the King broadcast his Christmas Day message to the nation.

Still, he did like his grub so there would be a dinner of sorts, Marianne assumed, so she went ahead and made a Christmas pudding. Gerald had a stir and she told him to make a wish, which he did, with his eyes screwed tightly shut.

Gradually Marianne found herself being drawn into the spirit of Christmas and she thought: why not decorate the hall? After all, there was no shortage of greenery and it would give an impression of goodwill even if there wasn't much of it in reality.

Of course, things would have been altogether different in Felicity's time. Marianne pictured her, flirtatious, glamorous, always the centre of attention, filling the house with guests and laughter and settling for nothing less than a tree that touched the ceiling.

Well there's nothing to stop us having a tree. She only had to say the word and Franz would chop one down for her. Already she could see it standing in the hall, glittering with tinsel and fairy lights.

Marianne gave the soup she was making a stir, tasted it, added seasoning, then left it to simmer while she checked the larder and made out a shopping list. She had on her coat ready to go out, when she heard the tap-tap of a stick on the hall tiles.

'Here comes trouble,' she muttered as Mrs Lacey limped into the kitchen. She stared at Marianne as if she suffered from some unspeakable affliction, then moved over to the kitchen range and lifted the lid on the saucepan.

'What's this?' she asked.

'Home-made vegetable soup, madam. I got a nice ham bone from the butcher's.'

'Well, actually I prefer Symingtons,' said Mrs Lacey, whose conciliatory manner following her son's drunken behaviour, had lasted for about two hours before reverting to type.

Marianne refused to react to the implied criticism of her cooking. 'You've had a bit of a cold, so I thought it would buck you up a bit.'

'Well, if there's nothing else I suppose it will have to do,' Mrs Lacey conceded in a martyred voice. 'Bring it up right away, will you?'

'I'm sorry, madam, but I'm just off to the village. The fish van comes at twelve and there's always a long queue. Captain Lacey is here tomorrow, remember.'

'Oh, yes. See that you get Dover sole; my son loves that.'

'I'll need more money, Dover sole is expensive.'

'I've none to spare.'

'It will have to be cod then, and if I don't get a move on, I'll be lucky to get that.'

'Well, did you get the cod?'

'No, four herrings and I had to queue for over a half hour in the freezing cold.'

'Oily horrible things, always repeat on me.'

'It was all the fishmonger had left.'

Mrs Lacey didn't answer but instead started fiddling with the dial on the wireless. As she watched her, Marianne began to think about Christmas decorations. If there were any in the house, the old lady would know where they were. On second thoughts perhaps not, Marianne decided, as she watched Mrs Lacey pick up the failing wireless and give it a good shake. If she finds out what I'm planning it'll give real pleasure to squash the idea stone dead.

'I think the accumulator needs recharging, madam,' Marianne pointed out, as Mrs Lacey continued to knock hell out of the radio. 'Shall I get it done for you?'

'No thank you.'

'Will that be all then, madam?'

'For the moment and close the door after you.' Later, when Marianne went to collect her tray, she found Mrs Lacey asleep and the wireless giving off a faint hum. Bliss! She could put her feet up and read a book until Gerald got home from school. Marianne turned off the radio and tiptoed to the door. She was almost through it when the dreaded voice spoke. 'Don't be in such a hurry. I've a job for you. I want you to give the billiard room a thorough clean. Friends might pop in over the Christmas period and my son will want to entertain them in there.'

Pop in? No one *pops* into this house, friends or otherwise. 'Right you are, madam.' Mine is not to reason why, Marianne recited to herself.

'And I shall be down later to inspect it,' the voice warned, 'so none of your usual slovenly flick with a duster.'

Oh Renée, please hurry up and come home and save me from this awful old woman, Marianne silently pleaded and dragged the vacuum cleaner into the billiard room.

Shortly after her arrival at Hope Grange Marianne had discovered that many of the rooms were closed off, the furniture shrouded in dust sheets. And for all it was used, this room might as well be too, she reflected as she polished the solid wooden legs of the billiard table, brushed down the green baize, and ran the vacuum cleaner over the parquet floor. But as she worked, to ease the boredom her fertile imagination began to fill the room with men in evening clothes, she heard the click of billiard balls, smelt rich Havana cigars. Marianne leaned on the vacuum cleaner and closed her eyes. There it was again, a woman's carefree laughter. What a wonderful place Hope Grange must have been in those far-off days.

'Have you finished?' The handsome men vanished and in front of her stood an elderly woman. 'Just about, madam,' Marianne replied; then, while her employer stood over her, she dusted the shaded lights that hung over the billiard table and wondered whether her obsession with the past was becoming a trifle unhealthy.

She had a word with Franz, who was more than happy to provide a Christmas tree and although Marianne was reluctant to admit that she was in competition with Felicity, to her mind a tree without decorations was pointless. And so the search began in drawers and cupboards, under beds and on top of wardrobes. Gradually she worked her way upstairs to the attic.

The midwinter light was poor, a bare bulb hung from a piece of wire and the inside of the skylight was filmed with ice. But gazing around the small cluttered room, Marianne realized that this was the natural home of discarded decorations and she'd bet anything they were in that tea chest over by the wall. However, it was empty save for a dead mouse. She moved on to a solid-looking trunk, but although there were no fairy lights or tinsel, stacked one on top of the other were what looked like photograph albums. Marianne took one from the top of the pile, blew off the dust and sat down in a rocking-chair. The cover was dark-blue tooled leather and embossed in gold across the front were the words, My Album. With the sense that this was a real find, Marianne undid the brass catch.

The first photograph, protected by a sheet of tissue paper, showed a woman in a crinoline and a small boy, wearing a velvet suit and with a mass of curls, leaning against her. Underneath the photograph was written: *My precious Hugo, aged seven years.* It seemed that the eldest male child was always given the name Hugo, except, of course, Gerald, and Marianne wondered why that was so, although there were no clues in the album. Subsequent photographs showed Hugo in a dog-cart, then as a grown man astride a hunter, and last of all standing stiffly beside his bride, surrounded by relatives and friends, all of them staring earnestly at the camera. Marianne studied the adult Hugo closely. Yes, underneath the whiskers he bore a strong resemblance to the present Hugo Lacey.

Making a quick assessment, Marianne reckoned there had to be a dozen or more albums. If they were all like this she'd struck gold, for they might solve the mystery of a young man's violent death, seemingly at the hands of a woman. She might also discover the whereabouts of her employer's wife, who seemed to have vanished into thin air.

'Armstrong, where are you?'

It was Gerald. Marianne slammed the album shut, shoved it back in the trunk, and threw a rug over it. She met Gerald halfway down the stairs. 'Yes, what is it you want?' she asked.

Gerald stared at her. 'You've got dirty streaks all down your face.'

Marianne gave her cheeks a rub with her apron. 'It must be the coal I brought in just now,' she lied.

'Can I have a cup of tea and one for Franz as well? And can you can bring it outside?'

Marianne was quite happy to make Franz tea, but not on the orders of Gerald. 'I'm not Franz's servant, you know.'

'But you are mine,' Gerald reminded her. He turned and ran down the stairs before Marianne could think of a suitably acid retort.

It was cold to the bone and the grey afternoon was slipping into darkness by the time Marianne took the tray of tea outside. It was official now, Mr Attlee and his government had bowed to the inevitable and she was no longer at risk of being thrown into jail for fraternizing with a POW. Not that it was a law to which Franz and Gerald had ever paid much attention. Pausing, Marianne watched them, perched on a tree trunk, chatting companionably and seemingly indifferent to the freezing temperature and approaching darkness. She didn't know how the German man achieved it, but in Franz's company Gerald was calmer, more biddable, and Marianne wished she'd been blessed with the German's particular gifts. She was also aware of Gerald's growing attachment to the young man. But he received so little affection from his father, it was almost inevitable. Nevertheless it made her a touch uneasy, for eventually Franz would be repatriated, leaving a vulnerable child to cope with yet another loss in his life. Maybe she ought to be doing something to loosen those ties, except that she hadn't the first idea how to set about it.

'You can't drink your tea out here, it's freezing. Why don't you come into the house?' Marianne offered, putting down the tray and rubbing her arms.

'The lorry will come to collect me soon, and we are tough soldiers, are we not, Master Gerald?' said Franz in his careful English. He ruffled the boy's hair affectionately.

'Yes, Franz, we are,' Gerald replied, staring up at him with a look bordering on adoration.

Although Marianne could understand Gerald's affection for Franz, her own response to him was more guarded, for there were still some unresolved issues to be dealt with, such as that Germans were killers, not gentle, unthreatening souls like Franz.

'Franz says we're going to have a white Christmas and I do hope so because he found a sledge in the stables and he says he's going to mend it for me.'

'Well I hope he's wrong. Coal is in short supply and it's hard enough keeping that house warm at the best of times.'

'I will saw up more logs for you,' Franz promised, 'then you will not be cold, Fräulein.'

'That would be a great help,' Marianne answered, remembering it was his job and so there was no need to sound grateful. Then, in an attempt to prise Gerald away she said, 'Coming to lock up the chickens with me?'

'No thank you.' Gerald moved closer to Franz and, seeing she wasn't going to win this one, Marianne left them drinking their tea.

The chickens were marvellous providers – when they were laying – and although they were silly, panicky creatures, she'd grown quite fond of them. After she'd secured them she stood for a while, listening to their soft chunterings and thinking fondly of Miss Webb and how she used to take her problems to her Rhode Island Reds.

A sadness swept over Marianne. Another person gone from her

life, marked only by a letter from the local doctor to say Miss Webb had died peacefully in her sleep. But she mustn't brood. With a resolute step she turned back to the house and was in time to see the pick-up lorry's tail light disappearing down the drive, followed by Gerald, calling and waving to Franz as if he couldn't bear to let him out of his sight.

Chapter Six

When Mrs Lacey's cold developed into what she claimed was influenza Marianne, guessing her employer would have her up and down the stairs ten times a day, decided to abandon preparations for Christmas for the time being.

'Would you like me to get the doctor to call?' Marianne suggested as her employer sneezed all over her.

'Certainly not.'

'He might give you some medicine for your chest.'

'I don't need medicine, I need looking after, something you have failed to do so far,' she snapped and proceeded to give Marianne the run around. Asserting her right as an invalid to do nothing for herself, Mrs Lacey demanded a commode in her room, which Marianne had to empty, calves' foot jelly to build up her strength, and oranges; some hopes. She also insisted on having her temperature taken night and morning even though the mercury never rose above normal.

Her bell rang incessantly, but if Marianne held out she sometimes gave up. Not this morning, however, and, her nerves frayed from overwork, Marianne snapped.

'Shut up!' she screamed and hurled a half-peeled potato at the row of bells. It missed and as it clumped to the ground, she saw that it was the front doorbell ringing.

The postman, with a Christmas parcel from Renée, it had to

be! Marianne gave a whoop of joy and skidded across the hall. But instead of the jovial Bob, a bowler-hatted stranger stood on the step.

'Can I help you?' She scowled at the man so fiercely, that he took a nervous step backwards, but recovered enough to hand her a card.

'I hope so. My name is Stoner, I'm from Petrie's Bank, and I wish to speak to Captain Lacey.'

'Captain Lacey's not here and won't be until Saturday.'

'Is there any other member of the family I might be able to see?'

'Mrs Lacey, his mother, but she's poorly.'

'Nothing serious, I trust.'

'Flu, she reckons.'

'I'd rather stay clear of that, but I hope she's soon on the mend.'

'So do I,' said Marianne with feeling. 'I'm run off my feet.'

'Oh dear.' Having dealt with the niceties, Mr Stoner went on, 'The bank has written to Captain Lacey on a number of occasions; he has received the letters, I assume?'

Marianne remembered the pile of unopened envelopes on Hugo Lacey's desk, which she occasionally dusted round. 'I only work here. Stuff comes through the letterbox all the time. But I don't pry.'

'Of course not. What time does Captain Lacey get home on a Saturday?'

'Late morning usually.'

'Have you a telephone?'

'If there was one it's been disconnected.'

'Will you give Captain Lacey my card and tell him I will be here at midday on Saturday and that it is most important that I speak to him. I must say this is the most wretched place to get to. I had to walk from the village and it will be Shanks's pony back,

I suppose.' He pursed his lips irritably, then stood back and surveyed the house.

'How many people live here?'

'Mr Lacey, his mother and son and me, for the time being.'

'In this great pile? Ridiculous when so many people who have been bombed out are still homeless.'

Marianne was inclined to agree with him.

'Now don't forget, I must see Captain Lacey on Saturday.'

'I'm only a servant; he gives the orders, not me, and I can't lock him up, so it might be another wild-goose chase. I reckon you'd have a better chance of finding him in if you turned up unexpectedly.' Marianne handed the card back to H. Stoner Esq. Assistant Bank Manager, and he gave her a knowing smile.

'How clever of you. I will indeed do that.'

'And if you ask at the pub, you can sometimes get a taxi up here,' Marianne advised as he turned to go.

H. Stoner lifted his bowler hat. 'Thank you, for your help, and I look forward to seeing you at the weekend.'

She would be the first to admit it, she was no genius when it came to figures, but having had her own money problems with the family, it wasn't difficult to work out why the bank was after Hugo Lacey, Marianne reflected as she invited Mr Stoner to step inside on the following Saturday.

'Wait here, please,' Marianne ordered and went to break the news to Hugo Lacey. 'There's a Mr Stoner here to see you, sir. Says he's from the bank.'

His expression darkened. 'Where is he?'

'In the hall.'

'You let him in?'

'I could hardly leave him outside, sir, it's snowing.'

'Put him in the billiard room, I'll speak to him there.'

It was clear that Mr Stoner hadn't come with good news so,

when the door had closed on the two men Marianne, taking the view that it was in her interest to know what was going on, lingered in the hall, nonchalantly flicking a feather duster around. She hadn't any idea what a captain's pay was, but it obviously wasn't enough to keep this house going. She was also cynical enough to know that it wouldn't be whisky or wine that was the first casualty if the money dried up, but her wages. Maybe she was being foolish in pinning her hopes on Renée, but her last letter had sounded really optimistic. 'I'll be home by March, sweetheart, and that's a promise, even if I have to swim the Atlantic'.

But this address was the only means of contact her aunt had with her, and behind the heavy doors voices were raised: Hugo Lacey's angry, Mr Stoner's more placatory. Giving up all pretence of dusting, Marianne pressed her ear against the door.

'It was my wife and her extravagances. And as you know, I have these other expenses. You must give me time. I'll sell off some of the—'

Mr Stoner's voice overrode the rest of the sentence and the only word she caught was, 'mortgage'. Then, abruptly, the door was wrenched open and Marianne shot back against the wall, hoping to make herself invisible. But the men were head to head like two bulls and oblivious to her.

'For the last time, Stoner, I am asking you to leave. Or do you want me to throw you out?' Giving the assistant bank manager the chance to depart with a little of his dignity still intact, Hugo Lacey handed him his rolled umbrella and bowler hat.

Shaken, Mr Stoner headed for the door. 'You haven't heard the last of this, Captain Lacey,' he warned. He tapped the bowler on to his head and got into a waiting taxi. Hardly five minutes later Hugo Lacey's car skidded off down the drive.

'That's goodbye to another week's wages,' Marianne predicted, and flung the feather duster across the hall.

'Was it you making all that commotion earlier, Armstrong?' Mrs Lacey snapped, when Marianne took up the daily paper.

'No; Captain Lacey and another gentleman, a Mr Stoner. He's from Petrie's Bank. They seemed to be having some sort of disagreement.' Marianne arranged Mrs Lacey's pillows so that she could sit up, and awaited her reaction.

'The bank?' The old lady's face shrivelled and she pushed the paper away. 'I don't want that, and stop fussing around me, girl.'

It was unheard of for Mrs Lacey not to do the crossword and, much as she disliked her, Marianne couldn't help pitying the woman. Renée wasn't going to turn up at any minute, so her own future was uncertain, but she was young and healthy and it would be easy enough to find another position. For Mrs Lacey, what beckoned? The workhouse?

On the following Monday Hugo Lacey turned up unexpectedly in a small van; then, with a grim expression, he marched through the house stripping the walls of paintings.

It took Marianne a while to work out what was going on, but when he started removing what remained of the porcelain figures from cabinets, she could no longer hold her tongue.

'What's happening, sir? What's happening?' she asked tearfully. But he continued his task in dogged silence and as soon as he'd wrapped and boxed the ornaments, he took them, and the paintings, out to the van and drove off without a word of explanation, even to his mother.

This wasn't the end of it because on the Tuesday afternoon a pantechnicon drove up to the front door. After letting down the back, two men in brown overalls followed Hugo Lacey into the house and then, on his directions, began removing furniture. Dumbfounded, Marianne stood and watched. The dining table and chairs went first, then the billiard table was dismantled and the legs, which she'd spent so much time polishing, were shouldered out through the door. The chaise longue was also on its way to a new home when a voice from above ordered, 'Put that down!' Then a bewildered old woman wailed, 'Hugo, what is going on?'

'Not out here, Mother,' Hugo Lacey warned. He raced up the stairs and guided his mother back into the bedroom.

'Well, looks like we might be kicking our heels for a while, Vic,' one of the removal men observed.

'Yeah. Any chance of a cuppa, m'dook?' Vic asked and parked himself down on the bottom step.

Although Marianne had no emotional attachment to Hope Grange, to her the men were like thieves stealing the life out of the house, so it was a relief to escape to the kitchen and make them tea. Outside the back door she could hear Franz stacking logs, and Marianne was about to fill the teapot when she was startled by a childish cry. Slamming down the kettle, she rushed out into the hall and found Gerald, his face puckered with distress, dragging on the coat of one of the removal men.

'That's my mother's and you shan't have it,' he screamed at the man, who was attempting to remove a lady's writing-desk from the house.

'Stop it, Gerald, this minute!' Hugo Lacey barked. He grabbed his son by the scruff of the neck and pulled him off. Normally Gerald was too much in awe of his father to question his authority, but Marianne could see that precious childhood memories were being snatched away from him.

Totally distraught, he turned on his father. 'It's all your fault!' he accused and fell upon him, pummelling him with his fists and aiming kicks at his legs with a fine precision.

'You little bastard!' His eyes blazing, Hugo Lacey lashed out with the back of his hand and sent Gerald sprawling across the tiled floor.

'Gerald, are you all right?' Marianne ran to him and lifted his head on to her lap. He was only slightly stunned, but she stared up at Hugo Lacey with disdain. 'You could have killed him.'

'Don't talk such tripe, woman,' he snarled, but it was clear by the way he ran his hands through his hair and did two complete circles, as if uncertain where he was, that her employer had reached breaking point.

Not sure what to make of it all, the removal men puffed nervously on their roll-ups. Eventually Vic pinched out his fag and stuck it behind his ear. 'Well, do we take the desk or not, guv?'

Hugo Lacey made a visible effort to pull himself together. 'I won't be dictated to by a child. Take it.' He flapped his hands to dismiss them.

'Right, Harold, off we go.'

Gerald was sitting up by the time the pantechnicon bumped off down the drive with his mother's desk in the back and his father in the front next to the driver and the other removal man, and his deeply felt misery wrenched at Marianne's heart.

As its sound faded, Franz put his head round the door. 'Anything wrong?'

Marianne was about to spill out the details, but Gerald beat her to it. 'No, I slipped and bumped my head, that's all.'

So that's how he wants to play it. No washing of dirty linen in public. Fair enough, thought Marianne.

'Will you give me a cuddle, Franz?'

'Of course.' Gerald held out his arms and Franz picked him up and carried him into the kitchen. He sat down with him in the fireside chair and Gerald curled his small body into Franz's as if he had every intention of remaining there for ever. As Marianne made tea, lavishly adding an extra spoonful of sugar to Gerald's cup, a thought struck her: that boy gets more affection from a German prisoner of war than he does from his own father.

Mrs Lacey recovered from the flu but not from the ransacking of her house and, although she had done her few favours, Marianne gained no pleasure in watching her physical decline. She also came to the conclusion that putting up a Christmas tree would be a mockery and would only accentuate the rattling emptiness of the house.

In spite of how she felt, Marianne found herself drawn increasingly to the attic, and the photograph albums and those pre-war optimistic times. In the end it became her sanctuary, the photographs an escape from a family falling apart. And she was comfortable in the company of these long-dead Laceys in their cumbersome clothes, primarily because she didn't have to bear the burden of their failures and, being dead, they couldn't disrupt her life.

Someone had gone to the trouble of dating the albums and this enabled Marianne to work her way through in them in a methodical fashion. Gradually she built up a picture of the family and from this she hoped to find out where it had all gone wrong for the Laceys.

As far as Marianne could make out, life had been good in those far-off days. There were marriages, christenings, but not too many of these because, as a family, they appeared not to be breeders. There were innumerable photographs of the family at leisure: picnicking, playing croquet, boating, starting out on the hunt or laying to waste what looked like the entire pheasant population of Leicestershire. In fact, an upper-class family enjoying the benefits of its wealth.

But it wasn't all sunshine and the face that stared up at her today was of a soldier standing beside his horse. The photograph was framed in black silk, and underneath was printed the name Julian. Under that, starkly, *Died in Action Crimea 1855.*

Marianne gently stroked the optimistic young face with her index finger. Poor Julian, so young to die. She turned over the page. An infant, swaddled in layers of clothes, lay it its cradle. The words: *Hermione, My Sweet One. With The Angels Now*, and a baby-fine curl pinned to the page, said everything and a lump rose in Marianne's throat. It was all so sad.

She thought of the absent, mysterious Felicity, remembered the grim words on the headstone in the graveyard, all a timely reminder that, rich or poor, every family had its share of grief and tragedy. After everything that had happened over the past days, it was too much for her to cope with. Marianne snapped the album shut and returned it to the trunk. They *would* have a fir tree, with or without decorations, Gerald deserved it, and as soon as she'd given the old lady her tea, she'd go and ask Franz to dig one up for them.

Chapter Seven

Muttering, 'Roll on spring,' Marianne pulled a third jumper over her head. But that was what...still three months away. She shouldn't be wishing her life away, she supposed, but in three months, with a bit of luck, Renée would be home, with Big Plans according to her last letter, the sun would start to warm the iron-clad earth, and the first snowdrop would appear. She hated these short days and the perpetual cold and, to cap it all, there were warnings of power cuts and Miss Hardcastle had run out of candles. Or so she claimed. Well, she might manage to pull the wool over some villagers' eyes, but Marianne knew that at the first power failure, candles would reappear on the shelves at double the price. There was a name for people like her, black marketeers, scum who profited from other people's misery. Well she'd better not try it on with me, Marianne thought darkly, because there are *laws*.

But it wasn't all gloom and doom. The tree was up, a *Tannenbaum* as Franz called it, standing in a galvanized bucket in the hall with silver stars and angels dangling from its branches, all cut out of sardine tins by Franz.

One frosty afternoon she roped in Gerald and the three of them went out into the grounds to gather fir-cones, holly, ivy and yew to decorate the hall. Gerald was in his element, shinning up trees, and then he'd gone too far, as he was inclined to do.

Leaning over the branch of an apple tree, he called, 'Look what I've got,' and dangled a bunch of mistletoe over their heads. 'Franz, you may kiss Armstrong now if you wish.'

Marianne blushed as red as the holly berries. 'No, he can't, and get down from that tree immediately,' she ordered.

'It was only a joke and everybody kisses under the mistletoe.'

'Not everyone. Apologize to Franz.'

'Sorry Franz.'

'It's all right, old chap, you have nothing to apologize for,' Franz answered, staring straight at Marianne.

One blush followed another. *The nerve.* He'll think I've got my eye on him. Well she would show him. 'Let's get this hall decorated,' she called up to Gerald, then, having gathered up an armful of greenery, Marianne marched off.

In case he should get any ideas, Marianne very pointedly ignored Franz and busied herself looping ivy along the mantelpiece and up the stairs. But as the gloomy hall was slowly transformed into a place of magic, she began to soften.

'Do you like?' Franz asked as they stood back to admire their efforts.

'It would look even better if we could have a fire in the hall, like we used to. It was the hugest one you've ever seen.' said Gerald.

'A half a hundredweight of coal was the most I could wangle from the coalman yesterday, so I've got to make it last.'

'But you have the logs, Fräulein,' Franz pointed out.

This brought to the surface a niggling worry. 'You know, I've a feeling that someone's stealing them. You keep me well supplied and I'm very careful, but there always seem to be fewer logs in the morning than there were the night before.'

'That must not happen.'

'How can I prevent it unless I sit up all night?'

'You must get a dog to guard them.'

Marianne laughed. 'A dog? Where from?'

'There is a poor creature that comes round the camp. I do not think he belongs to anyone because he is always hungry. I could build him a kennel, put it by the back door and he would frighten away thieves.'

Marianne thought about Franz's suggestion. The logs were as precious as gold nuggets and, by the looks of it, likely to become more so. Without them she would be unable to cook or keep the house even minimally warm. 'I'll have a word with Mr Lacey.'

'Out of the question,' her employer bellowed when she put the idea to him. However, he quickly changed his tune when Marianne told him of her suspicions.

'How dare some criminal come on to my property and steal,' he boomed, getting quite hot under the collar. 'Certainly get a dog, and to teach those thieves a lesson, make sure it's a ferocious beast with fangs that'll rip their throats out.'

So, a day later, a large dog arrived in the lorry with Franz.

'This is Boris,' said Franz introducing him.

Marianne laughed. 'Who gave him that name?'

'One of the guards. He said he's Boris Karloff's double.'

With his long ears, dewlaps and lugubrious expression, Marianne would have said he resembled an elderly judge rather than a famous film star. 'Hello Boris,' she said, leaning towards him. His tail gave an uncertain thump, and his soulful eyes pleaded with her to approve.

'He doesn't seem very ferocious.'

'But your bark, it is very loud, is it not, Boris?'

Marianne could have sworn the dog nodded. 'Well, you'd better get on with finishing his kennel then, and something will have to be done about his coat, it looks as if someone's been using him as a doormat,' she said and went to fetch the bone she'd scrounged off the butcher.

For the rest of the morning Marianne heard nothing but hammering and sawing; then at midday Franz came struggling down with what looked like a small house. Immediately Boris went and sat in it, paws crossed and king of all he surveyed. However when Gerald came tearing up the drive shouting excitedly, 'Is he here, is the dog here?' Boris was out of the kennel in a second, hackles raised and standing guard.

'Don't let him bite me!' Gerald, shrieked, and flung himself against Franz.

'He will not bite you, he is doing his job and guarding his territory, but you must speak quietly to him. Come here, boy.' Franz slapped his thigh and the dog advanced, tail wagging. 'Say "hello Boris", and hold out your hand,' Franz ordered and gave the boy a slight push. But as Boris began sniffing around him, Gerald went rigid.

'Now stroke him.'

Gerald patted the dog nervously, Boris reached up and licked his face and a tentative friendship was struck up.

'He needs a bath, so why don't you take him up to the stables and see to it?' Marianne suggested.

'All right. Come on, Boris.'

'I think they will soon be good friends,' said Franz as they watched boy and dog run off together.

'Thank you for bringing Boris, I feel safer now.'

After this Gerald would spend hours grooming the dog, although almost immediately Boris would rush out, find the dirtiest part of the garden and roll around in it with doggy grunts of delight.

A couple of nights after his arrival, Marianne woke to ferocious growls and barking, followed by curses and running feet. Good boy, thought Marianne, he was proving his worth, their fuel supplies were safe. Reassured, she turned over and went back to sleep.

*

'The hall and the tree look splendid, Armstrong. Congratulations,' said her employer as he handed over her wages the following Saturday.

'Yes, Master Gerald's getting very excited. Christmas morning can't come soon enough, and he's so looking forward to his presents.'

Hugo Lacey cleared his throat. 'Oh yes ... er ... presents.'

'A Meccano set is top of his list,' Marianne prompted.

'Ah, excellent, just what I've got him.'

'Can we also talk about Christmas dinner, sir.'

He scowled at her. 'Money, money, money. Spend, spend, spend, that's all Christmas amounts to these days. The real meaning's gone out of it.'

Marianne braced herself. It had to be said. 'Actually I was wondering where you plan to eat now that there's no dining table.'

He looked slightly taken aback at her bluntness, thought for a moment and then answered, 'Dammit, we'll eat in here. At least it's warm.'

'Right you are, sir,' Marianne answered and had a little smile to herself. Wait until Mother hears she's got to sit and eat amongst the pots and pans. 'And will we be having something special or just the normal roast?'

Hugo Lacey gave an airy wave of the hand. 'Definitely something special, a goose or turkey, and I promise you I'll have it here in good time, so don't worry yourself on that score.'

He was as good as his word. Almost. He came through the door, ebullient, half-drunk, on the afternoon before Christmas Eve and dumped a leg of pork on the table.

'Christmas dinner,' he announced, pulled out a chair, sat down and drew a bottle of whisky from his greatcoat pocket.

Marianne stared at the meat. 'Where'd you get that from, sir?' Poultry wasn't rationed, pork definitely was.

He tapped the side of his nose, and gave her a secretive smile. 'Best not to ask.' Which meant the pig had been slaughtered illegally. Well, he was the one who'd be fined if it came to light, Marianne reflected. But as she put it on a serving dish and placed it in the larder, her mouth was already watering: crackling, sage-and-onion stuffing, apple sauce, she couldn't wait.

'Oh, and Armstrong, I was wondering...' he paused and blinked ... 'if you would oblige me by taking Gerald to the Christmas Eve service at St John's.'

Marianne pushed shut the larder door with her foot and swung round. 'I do have rather a lot to do on Christmas Eve, sir,' she said severely. 'Stuffing to make, vegetables to prepare.'

Marianne watched him pour a drink. *Of course, being a toff you think it all happens by magic, don't you?*

'Care for one?' He held up the bottle.

Marianne shook her head.

'You don't know what you're missing.' He gulped back his drink and went on, 'This is a bit of a special occasion. You see, Gerald is singing in the choir, and I don't want to let the vicar down.'

Never mind about the vicar, what about your son? 'I'm sure Gerald would prefer to have you there.' All those dewy-eyed parents and there was the poor little devil having to make do with a servant, again. She wondered how he could be so indifferent to his son's feelings.

'I'd love to go, I really would, but duty calls.'

Yeah, some floozy. Marianne wished she had the courage to confront him with these so-called duties. 'What about Mrs Lacey, can't she take him?'

'My mother is becoming rather frail.'

He was right; she grew more wizened by the day, like a tortoise retracting into its shell.

Hugo Lacey pushed five crisp one-pound notes across the table and Marianne thought of the sales. They started in Leicester just after New Year and she could really do with a warm winter coat and some fur-lined boots. And she and Miss Webb had never missed the Christmas Eve service, and it did have a timeless magic, even for a fainthearted Christian like herself.

While she dithered, two more notes followed. Putting all scruples behind her, Marianne snatched them up. 'Well … perhaps I could get the vegetables and stuffing done in the afternoon …'

'Good girl.' He stood up and made off in the general direction of the door, had a tussle with the handle, then tottered out into the hall.

Marianne shook her head. There was the rest of the day and tomorrow to get through yet and the question was: would he be sober or legless by Christmas day?

'He'd only make me feel nervous then I'd probably sing out of tune, so I'm glad he's not coming,' was Gerald's only reaction when Marianne explained to him that, although his father desperately wanted to hear him sing, important matters prevented him.

What a sad reflection of their relationship, Marianne thought, as Gerald went off to change and she found herself a place in a pew halfway down the church. But of course Franz was filling the gap, providing the affection, becoming the father figure, and bringing with it other problems.

Marianne bent her head, made a brief appeal to God to send Renée home soon, and then looked about her. Apart from a few empty places at the front, the church was full. The organ played softly, candles burned in the windows, baby Jesus lay in his manger surrounded by humble beasts of the field and Marianne felt herself succumbing to the mystery and magic of Christmas. And then the tranquillity was shattered by the sound of marching feet and she, and the rest of the congregation, turned to stare as a dozen or more POWs filed self-consciously down the aisle to the front pews.

Among the group was Franz; as he passed he gave Marianne a brief smile. The church was now full, the doors were closed and the vicar took his place at the chancel steps. Then the organ began to play, 'Once in Royal David's City,' and a lone boy's voice, pure and true, soared to the arched roof of the church. As the choir processed down the aisle Marianne was astonished to see that it was Gerald, looking angelic in his choirboy ruffle and blue surplice. By now she had a lump in her throat and a tear in her eye. How could a father miss this, his son's proudest moment? But it was Christmas Eve and she must not let discord enter into her heart. Clearing her throat, Marianne joined the congregation in singing the final verses of the carol.

Various leading lights of the village then went into the pulpit and read verses relating to the Christmas story, after which the vicar announced that, as a gesture of friendship and goodwill, the prisoners of war would sing for them.

To murmurs of surprise the men stood and faced the congregation; then, with one of them strumming on a guitar, they began to sing: *Stille Nachte, heilige Nacht* ... Silent Night, Holy Night ... first in German, then English. The candles flickered, the air smelt of wax and evergreen, and Marianne watched Franz closely. His face was etched with the raw pain of homesickness, although, like her, he was an orphan with no home to go to. She'd discovered this one afternoon over a cup of tea and cigarette. 'And what do you hope to do when you're repatriated?' she asked, after she'd finished explaining that Renée was the only reason she stayed on at Hope Grange.

Franz had stretched proudly and replied, 'I will become a teacher like my father.' And then the appalling story came spilling out, how before the war his father had run a school for crippled children, until Hitler came to power with his dream of a master race. On the Nazi party's orders the school was closed and the children taken away, to where, his father could only guess. But he never gave up trying to find them and his persistence landed him in prison. When he was eventually released he was so broken in spirit that he died within a month. Franz heard of his mother's death through the Red Cross, while he was a prisoner in America. There were no brothers or sisters and all he had to return to was a divided, shattered country. What with Gerald's singing, then the men's, and the whole astonishing atmosphere of forgiveness in the church, Marianne was all raw emotion and a tear traced its way down her cheek. And at that exact second, with a click, a door in her heart opened and she let Franz in.

Overwhelmed, Marianne remembered little after this, although she probably mouthed her way through the rest of the carols. She did remember to wait outside for Gerald, though, where the congregation was crowding around the young Germans with invitations to join them for Christmas dinner.

Slightly bewildered by their generosity the men smiled and thanked them, then Gerald tugged at Marianne's hand. 'Why don't you ask Franz to come and have dinner with us?'

'Can you imagine your father's reaction?'

'I shall invite him then.'

Marianne grabbed his arm. 'You will not.'

Franz was now glancing in their direction and, after murmuring something to one of his companions, he moved over to speak to them.

'The Lord has given you a beautiful voice, Gerald. Hasn't he?' he asked, turning to Marianne.

But love was new to her and with all the unfamiliar emotions flooding through her, Marianne didn't dare look at him; all she could manage was a pathetic 'Y ... y ... yes.'

Gerald, however, had plenty to say for himself. '*She* won't let me ask you to dinner tomorrow,' he accused, lapsing rapidly from the saintly to the diabolical.

Marianne looked up, saw the hurt on Franz's face and found her voice. 'It's not like that at all. It would have to be Mr Lacey's decision and he's not here.'

'I won't see you for two whole days,' Gerald accused tearfully.

'But you've got Boris,' Marianne reminded him and noticed the vicar bearing down on them.

'Has anyone invited you into their home yet, young man?' he asked Franz.

Franz glanced at Marianne, 'No, Father.'

'Then you must come and share our meal.'

Franz clicked his heels together and gave a small bow. 'You are very kind.'

'Holy Communion is at nine a.m. I will see you after church. And don't worry, several of your comrades are joining us and we'll try and make it a happy day for you all.'

He bid them goodnight and as he walked off, Franz was smiling. 'These are good people, taking us into their homes.'

'Yes, and we must go. It's a long walk and your friends are waiting for you.' And talking about us, thought Marianne, noticing how they kept glancing in their direction.

Indifferent to the other men, Franz lifted his hand and lightly touched her cheek. '*Frohliche Weinachten, meine Liebling*,' he murmured tenderly.

'Happy Christmas, Franz,' Marianne replied and, smiling up at him, she offered him her love.

Chapter Eight

Although there was every likelihood she'd be accused of extravagance, Marianne lit the fire in the hall on Christmas morning. She wasn't in competition with Felicity, she told herself, but Mrs Lacey, ignoring the sad fact that the family had received only one Christmas card, spoke of friends dropping in. Curious to know who the card was from, Marianne took it down from the mantelpiece. On the front a fat porker pranced around on its hind legs and inside Mr Veal thanked them for their esteemed custom and wished them a prosperous New Year. That must be some sort of sick joke. The butcher's shop was the equivalent of the village pump and Mr Veal was bound to be fully up to date on the comings and goings of bankers, auctioneers and removal vans.

In the days leading up to Christmas Marianne had worried that the captain, never a man to put his son before a bottle of whisky, would reach down into his pockets and find them empty. So it was with a sense of relief that she saw that, overnight, a few parcels had been placed under the tree.

Marianne added her own gift, a Laurel and Hardy Annual, and at the same time took a squint at the labels. She recognized Mrs Lacey's shaky handwriting on one, and another was inscribed: *To Gerald with best wishes for Christmas, Father.* A bit formal, but at least he'd remembered and so had Franz. Marianne picked up the parcel and for the sheer pleasure of it on her tongue, said out loud, 'Franz. Franz whom I love.'

A sort of blissful derangement had carried her home the night before, kicking up snow, singing at the top of her voice, until Gerald had enquired in a censorious tone, 'Are you drunk or something, Armstrong?'

She wanted to shout, 'Yes, yes, drunk with love.' Instead she answered scornfully, 'Of course not,' and felt her cheek. It still burned where Franz's fingers had caressed it, but she had to be careful, because amorous fraternization was still frowned upon. Then an appalling thought struck her; maybe she was reading things into an innocent gesture. Chastened by this possibility, Marianne finished the walk home in a more sedate manner.

She slept fitfully, and was awakened by the doorbell being tugged. She pulled on a skirt and jumper and ran downstairs to answer it. As she pulled back the bolts, across the snowy wastes Marianne could hear church bells and closer, the complaining voice of the postman. 'If I gets a hernia from cycling up here with this bloomin' great thing, I shall hold you responsible, young lady,' he admonished and dumped a parcel in Marianne's arms.

Although she nearly buckled under the weight of it, Marianne managed to check whom it was for. 'It's a Christmas present for me, from my aunt in America,' she said proudly, and offered Bob a mince pie.

'I wouldn't say no. And it'll help me keep my energy up until I gets home to the little 'uns and me missus.'

'Hold on a sec.' Marianne struggled into the kitchen, dumped the parcel on the table and, in a fit of generosity, returned with two mince pies. Bob thanked her, stuffed one into his mouth then, while chewing, gave her a detailed description, including the price, of every present he'd bought his children. Three times as much as Hugo Lacey had spent on his son by Marianne's reckoning. He finished the second mince pie, wiped his mouth and, with a farewell wave, sped off home to his family.

Marianne returned the wave; then, with a sense of anticipation, hurried back to the kitchen. Delaying gratification, she stood admiring the size and solidness of the parcel, while trying to imagine what was inside. Well, only one way to find out, she told herself, and began to unknot the miles of string and smooth out the strong brown paper for future use. Eventually she took a knife to the cardboard box and slashed it open. As she foraged amongst the straw packaging Marianne was reminded of those bran tubs at fêtes, except that the prizes she was pulling out were worth having: tins of butter, pineapple chunks, fruit salad, sliced peaches, Spam, and about a dozen Hershey bars. What a feast, but for her and Gerald and Franz only. As she dug deeper, Marianne found more stuff, four pairs of nylons, and several copies of the *Saturday Evening Post*. The front cover of one showed a smiling, well-fed family sitting around a table, the centrepiece of which was an enormous turkey, to which Father was about to take a carving knife. A bit different from family life in this household, Marianne reflected and put the magazines aside to read later. She dug around a bit more for the letter she knew would be there, heard the crackle of cellophane and pulled out a package with a note pinned to it.

Hi ya kid! Typical Renée, Barely a year and already acting like a Yank.
You know how Nan liked us well turned out and I don't expect you have much chance to put on weight with the amount of food you get in England, so the dress should fit. It's real wool too, and warm. As it's Christmas, I chose green, and I can just see you in it, looking so pretty all the chaps will go goggle-eyed. Doing two jobs now and a bit pushed for time, but want to get this parcel off, or you'll think I've forgotten you. Weather lousy

in NY so, like the swallows, I'm flying south to Florida, where I'm hoping it'll be warmer. Don't worry, it's only temporary and I've got most of my fare saved for the passage home, which will be pretty soon. Have a happy Christmas. Next year we'll spend it together. All my love, Renée.

'Promises, promises.' Marianne sighed, and pulled open the cellophane package. *I have to be practical, I'm not going to see my aunt ever again.* She took the dress from its wrapping, held it in front of her and immediately forgave her aunt. The clever girl *had* got the size right – and the colour.

Boris was now scratching at the door. Marianne went and let him in. 'What do you think, do I look pretty?' she asked him, but Boris's thoughts were of the most basic kind: food and warmth, and he made a beeline for the fire.

'Don't think you can lounge around here today, young man,' Marianne admonished, placing a saucer of tea and the remains of her toast in front of him. 'You'll get in my way while I'm cooking and you were hired as a guard dog. The captain will want to see you out there, earning your keep.'

It was her fault, she knew, that Boris was growing indolent and used to the indoor life, but she enjoyed his company and he was someone to talk to even if the conversation was one-sided. Also, like all dogs, he knew a softy when he saw one, and as he finished his breakfast and settled down again, Marianne weakened. 'Oh all right, but you go in the broom cupboard at twelve.' This was Boris's hidy hole and whenever he heard the captain's footsteps he would creep off in there.

She wrapped a couple of Hershey bars for Gerald and was putting them with the rest of the presents when he came racing down the stairs, still in his dressing-gown and slippers.

When he saw the fire blazing away in the hearth, he stopped. 'You've lit the fire.'

'Cheers the place up, don't you think?' answered Marianne.

But Gerald was now focused on the Christmas tree, and the presents underneath. He fell to his knees and started ripping them open. 'Oh good, just what I wanted, a Meccano set – and a Bible from Grandmother,' he added, but with less enthusiasm; then he opened Marianne's present. 'Thank you, Armstrong, how did you know I liked Laurel and Hardy?' he asked, stuffing chocolate into his mouth.

'You mentioned it once.'

'They're putting on some flicks at the village hall next week. Will Hay one night, Laurel and Hardy the next. Will you take me?'

'I don't see why not, if your pa doesn't mind.'

'All he minds is that I don't bother him.'

Out of the mouths of babes and sucklings, thought Marianne and watched Gerald undo his last present, the one from Franz. 'Gosh, a square-rigger,' he said and held it up for her to see.

Marianne studied her beloved's handiwork. 'Why it's beautiful. And just look at the detail. It must have taken him hours, weeks. He really must think an awful lot of you, going to all that trouble.'

'Franz will go back to Germany one day, won't he?'

'Yes, it's his home.' Marianne felt a tightness in her throat.

'Does that mean we'll never see him again?'

Gerald was asking questions she didn't dare contemplate. Yesterday Franz had been a friend, today he was the man she loved, and his going out of her life was something she was unwilling to confront just now. 'Oh I shouldn't think so, I'm sure he'll come back and visit us one day,' she answered brightly.

'I shall ask him to take me with him.'

It was Christmas, not a day on which a child should be expected to face reality, so all she said was, 'All right, but in the meantime, could you go and get dressed. And I think it would be

95

a nice gesture if you took breakfast up to your grandmother while I get on with dinner. You'll be able to thank her for her present as well.'

'I'll go after I've said hello to Boris,' Gerald replied, getting his priorities right.

Left on her own, depression descended like a lead balloon, creeping up on her while she was putting the leg of pork into the oven, then as she stirred the custard and lastly set the table. Eventually Marianne came to the sad conclusion that, like all the other people she'd loved, Franz was destined to play only a brief part in her life. It was as if she was pursued by some awful curse.

'All those delicious aromas.'

The voice cut through Marianne's self-pity and she turned from basting the potatoes. Hugo Lacey was wearing civvies: flannel trousers, a check shirt with a cravat tucked into the neck and a navy-blue blazer. He looked handsome and amiable, in fact, Jack Buchanan personified. *Women must fall over themselves until they find out about his drinking and violence.*

'I should have dinner on the table by one. Will you be carving, sir?' Marianne asked, thinking that, at least for today, they could have a shot at being a happy, united family, like that one on the front cover of the magazine.

He laughed. 'Good heavens, definitely not. I'll leave that in your capable hands, Armstrong.'

'I take it that Mrs Lacey knows she's eating in the kitchen?'

'Probably not.'

'She might not like the idea, so could you warn her?'

'I'll go and tell her now. By the way, you must eat with us today.'

'But I couldn't … your mother wouldn't care for it at all.'

'I insist, and my mother will have to try and remember that it's the season of goodwill.'

Since Mrs Lacey had never shown a trace of goodwill towards

her, Marianne thought it unlikely she'd start today. However, she did want the day to go smoothly, so after checking that the crackling on the pork was crisping nicely and that the Christmas pudding wasn't about to boil dry, she raced upstairs to change, reasoning that if she looked less like a servant Mrs Lacey might find it easier to tolerate her.

The dress Renée had sent fitted a treat and the skirt, which had yards of material in it, swirled out around her nylon-clad legs. Marianne sized herself up in the cracked mirror. Not bad, she decided, slipped her feet into her red shoes, painted her lips a bold red to match and ran downstairs, pleased with her appearance.

Before she started to carve the meat and make the gravy, Marianne enveloped herself in a large white pinny, only taking it off when she went into the hall to bang the gong.

With his mother on his arm, Hugo Lacey descended the stairs only a little less unsteady on his feet than his mother. Gerald followed, looking sullen, and Marianne's heart sank. *Some dinner this is going to be.*

Hugo Lacey stared at her but said nothing; Mrs Lacey peered disdainfully. 'Too much lipstick and those red shoes remind me of that whore.'

'Mother!' her son reprimanded her, and Marianne's cheeks flared in anger.

'I'm sorry, Armstrong. My mother gets confused at times; she doesn't mean it,' Hugo apologized in a low voice and walked on into the kitchen. He helped his mother into her seat and, not yet done with poisoning the occasion, Mrs Lacey gazed about her. 'I never thought I'd live to see this, our family eating in the kitchen.' Her voice trembled with anguish.

'I always eat in here, Grandmama, it's the warmest place in the house. That's 'cos of Franz, who saws up lots of logs for us.'

'Are you talking about that Nazi who hangs around the place?'

Marianne, who was putting the vegetable dishes on the table, flinched. Would nothing stop this woman? 'Franz is not a Nazi, madam.'

'No, they never are. If they were all so opposed to Hitler, why didn't they do something about it?'

'Franz's father tried and he was put in prison. And then he died.'

'Well, he'd tell you that, wouldn't he? You're the gullible sort that would swallow his lies.'

The muscles in Marianne's face were so taut she had trouble speaking. 'Master Gerald, show your grandmother the sailing ship Franz made for you.'

Gerald slid down from his chair and went to get it. 'Isn't it a beauty, Grandmama?' He held it up for her to admire. Mrs Lacey peered at it but made no comment, neither did her son, but then he was pulling the cork out of a wine bottle and there were priorities.

Marianne divided the meat and the stuffing between four plates then a little uncertainly joined the family at the table.

'I really cannot stand these indignities, Hugo, I will eat in my room.' Mrs Lacey went to stand but Hugo pushed her back down.

'You will not, Mother. It is Christmas Day and I invited Armstrong to join us.'

Marianne picked up her plate and cutlery. She couldn't face any more dissent. 'I can eat later—'

Hugo Lacey thumped the table. 'Is no one listening to me?'

Marianne, who was close to breaking point, sat down again and took several gulps from her glass, now filled with white wine, and felt better. She was as near to purgatory as she'd ever been and she needed the wine to get her through today. The meal proceeded in silence except for the clicking of Mrs Lacey's jawbone. The food she'd prepared with such care tasted like straw in Marianne's mouth.

She took several more gulps of wine to help the food down, and was surprised to see she'd emptied the glass. Hugo Lacey immediately refilled it. Well, there was something to be said for wine, Marianne mused as she threw it down, at least it got you through impossible situations. What Mrs Lacey thought of her no longer mattered one jot.

Marianne finished the food on her plate and stood up. 'Who's for second helpings?' she asked, and Gerald and his father both held out their plates.

A cork was pulled from another bottle. Then, as Marianne was placing the Christmas pudding and the custard on the table, several small glasses appeared along with a bottle of Benedictine.

'There's a threepenny bit in there for some lucky person,' Marianne said, as she divided up the pudding, which she was pleased to see was rich and dark and moist.

And of course it had to be Mrs Lacey who got the small coin. 'Do you want me to crack my teeth on it, you stupid girl?' she accused, and spat it out on the plate in disgust. 'I'm sorry, Hugo, but I've had just about as much as I can take. A minute more and I'll collapse, so I have to ask you to take me to my room.' Placing her palms on the table to support herself she, stood up.

'All right, Mother.' Her son's tone was one of weary resignation.

'Well, no point in wasting it,' said Gerald as soon as they'd gone. He reached out for his grandmother's leftovers, and at the same time pocketed the threepenny piece.

'I don't know why I bother. I worked my socks off trying to make it nice for everyone today and I get nothing but insults from your grandmother,' said Marianne tiredly. Then she dropped her head on the table and wept.

'Never mind about her, Armstrong, you gave us a marvellous meal and I really enjoyed it, so did my father.'

A small hand patted her back and Marianne raised her head. 'You're right, he did.' She sniffed and wiped her eyes.

'Tell you what, why don't we go tobogganing? There's a smashing slope over near Frog Lane.'

'What, with all the pots to do? How can I?'

'You've got all evening.' Gerald pointed out. 'I'll give a hand.'

Marianne looked sceptical. This was a boy who never lifted a finger. 'You?' But she was coming round to the idea. An hour or two away from the oppressive atmosphere of the house would do wonders for her health.

'I promise.'

Marianne stood up. 'Right, I'm holding you to that. But you'd better ask your father first, see if he's agreeable.'

'Okey dokey.'

'And don't let him hear you using slang, or he certainly won't let you go,' Marianne called after him.

While she waited Marianne scraped the leftovers into Boris's dish and by the time Gerald returned, he'd licked it clean. 'The answer's yes and can we take Boris?' said Gerald in one breath.

Hearing his name, Boris's ears gave an expectant twitch.

'Why not? A run'll do him good.' Marianne put the remains of the joint in the larder, left the plates and cutlery to soak and, while she went to change into her slacks, Gerald got out the recently repaired sledge.

'So how far is it to Frog Lane?' Marianne asked, as they set off.

'Couple of fields away,' Gerald answered, adding, 'Look at Boris.' He started to laugh as the dog sniffed around in the snow, nose to the ground like a bloodhound, but stopping every now and then to cock his leg against a tree and turn the snow yellow.

Gradually Marianne unwound, and the tension that had gripped her after sitting through that awful meal eased. It was such a joy to get away from the house, even if she occasionally found herself sinking into a snowdrift. Also there was a smoky orange sun and the air was as crisp as an apple. Against all the odds, Marianne had a bizarre feeling that things would turn out all right for her.

The two fields turned into three, then four but at last Marianne heard screams and laughter. Gerald called, 'Nearly there,' and a moment later they were staring down a very steep slope.

'Get on,' Gerald ordered, and dumped himself down on to the sledge.

But Marianne backed away. 'No fear, I don't want my neck broken.'

Gerald gave a shrug, spread himself along its length, then hurtled, head first down the hill at a speed that made Marianne fear for his life. But others were doing it and surviving: kids on dustbin lids, POWs on pieces of corrugated iron. In fact there was such a happy, carefree atmosphere that Marianne began to regret her cowardice. And she hadn't seen so many people in one place since Bonfire night. She noticed too that, like young men anywhere, the Germans were flirting with the village girls, even offering them rides on their make-do sledges. Knowing the rules and fearful of their reputations, some girls held back, but there were bolder ones, game for anything and off they went, clasped in the arms of a young man who, until recently, had been a sworn enemy. Well, love makes the world go round, so good luck to them, thought, Marianne. But she couldn't help feeling envious and she wished Franz were here instead of at the vicarage.

As she thought this there was a sharp whistle, Boris's ears twitched, then he shot off, his rump wiggling like Carmen Miranda's, and as the cause of all this doggy excitement walked towards her, Marianne's heart began to beat in double time.

Franz took her gloved hand and squeezed it. How are you, *meine Liebling?*'

'Happy to see you.' Marianne smiled up at him shyly, then blushed at her boldness.

And then Gerald was there, pushing between them, tugging at

Franz's coat and spoiling their shared moment. 'Franz, Franz, you must come on the sledge, it's brilliant.'

'First I go with Marianne.'

'It's no good asking her, she's a scaredy-cat.'

'Scaredy-cat?' Franz repeated.

'He means I'm a coward.'

'But you will not be with me looking after you.'

Marianne took a step back. 'No, no sorry, I can't.'

Franz shrugged, and Marianne knew he'd taken it personally. He thinks I'm ashamed to be seen with him because he's a German, because he's shabby, because I'm worried about my good name, but nothing could be further from the truth, she thought, watching the two of them hurl themselves off into space. And why can't I just relax and have fun like everyone else, instead of standing here like a timorous mouse?

The extreme cold and fading light were sending people home. In a short while it would be dark. *If I'm going to show Franz I'm not rejecting him, I'll have to do it now.* Marianne braced herself, watched them scramble back up the hillside, then called out bravely, 'I will have a go.'

'Gut,' Franz answered; then, before she changed her mind, he sat her down on the sledge and tucked himself in around her Reassured by his strong heartbeats, Marianne relaxed.

'Off we go and do not be frightened,' he said comfortingly, Gerald gave them a shove and they went skimming down the slope at what seemed like the speed of light. Marianne screamed in terror. She would never survive. As she thought this, she felt a violent jolt to her spine and the sledge flipped over, tossing them both into the snow. Marianne found herself on her back, still alive with Franz gazing down at her. 'We hit a stone. Are you all right?'

'I think so. What about you?'

'Better than I've ever been,' Franz answered, then he bent and kissed her. In spite of the cold his lips were warm, but Marianne held back for a minute, thinking, I'll be the talk of the village. But as Franz's kisses became more persistent, she wound her arms round his neck and responded with a shy delight.

'Oh my little Marianne, I can hardly believe this,' Franz murmured, and was about to kiss her again when a childish voice demanded, 'What are you two doing lying in the snow?' A moment later Gerald was standing over them and Marianne found herself at the receiving end of Boris's exuberant kisses instead of those of the man she loved.

But she was so happy it didn't matter and, seeing the funny side of it, she started to laugh and so did Franz, then Gerald, while Boris got all silly and chased his tail.

After long moments Franz took Marianne's hand. 'We cannot lie here, or we will turn into blocks of ice.' As he brought her to her feet, he pulled her close and said quietly, 'You are my sweetheart, yes?'

'I am your sweetheart, yes,' Marianne repeated solemnly.

'Stop whispering,' Gerald ordered, and Marianne knew that his jealousy could easily throw up all sorts of problems in the future. However, Franz was careful not to exclude him and taking Gerald's hand and hers, together they scrambled back up the icy slope. Reaching the top, they paused for breath. The only people left on the slopes were POWs. Gerald greeted them all by name, while Boris came in for a great deal of attention, and Marianne recognized them as the contingent that drove up in the lorry each day.

A conversation in German followed, then Franz turned to Marianne and Gerald. 'My friends, they would like to invite you and Gerald and Boris back to the camp for cocoa.'

Taken aback by the offer, Marianne answered, 'But how would we get past the guards?'

'Now that we are allowed out they do not take much notice, but we will go in the back way, under the barbed wire.'

'But if we get caught?'

'That will not happen,' Franz answered with absolute certainty, which made Marianne think that perhaps they weren't the first to be smuggled into the camp.

'Oh please, let's go,' Gerald implored.

'All right, as long you promise not to breathe a word to your father.'

'Of course I won't.'

It turned out to be quite simple getting into the camp. Boris went with the men through the main gate; Marianne, Franz and Gerald squeezed in under the barbed wire, although Marianne's heart was beating with terror.

Inside the Nissen hut Franz very formally invited them to sit down. Curious, and eager to know everything about the man she loved, Marianne relaxed and looked around. The hut was a large half-cylinder of corrugated iron with a cement floor, bunk beds ran down either side and there was a stove in the middle with a chimney going up through the roof.

Turning back to Franz, she asked, 'Where do you sleep?'

'Over here.' Taking her hand, he led her to a neatly laid out bed. On the wall was a photograph of a man and woman, arms linked and smiling.

'*Mein Vater und Meine Mutter.*' Marianne caught the desolation in his voice. 'And soon we will be going home.'

Marianne swung round. 'Oh no. When?'

'A month, two months, I am not sure.'

'You can't go,' she wailed, 'not now.'

'I do not wish it, but I have no choice.'

Behind her Marianne could hear the men teaching Gerald to sing in German. 'Please don't saying anything to Gerald, it will break his heart.'

'And mine is breaking too.'

'Oh Franz, what shall we do?'

He had no answer for her and the chief cocoa-maker was calling them over. Marianne sipped hers and felt sick. She was also nervous and convinced that the camp commandant would shortly walk through the door.

'I think we should go, Franz.'

Gerald started to make a fuss, until the men reassured him he could come again, and he chattered about this all the way home. With the parting hanging over them, Marianne and Franz were silent. When they reached the back door, Franz checked the logs. 'They are going down, so I will come tomorrow and saw up some more. *Gute Nacht.*' He squeezed her hand and gave her a quick kiss.

'Good night, Franz,' Gerald answered. Marianne couldn't speak; she just stood and watched him walk away. When he'd disappeared into the darkness of the trees, she turned and went into the house, thinking: I've found love and almost immediately I've got to prepare myself for losing Franz.

Gerald paused to pull off his wellington boots, then ran through to the hall.

Marianne dashed after him. 'Hey, what about the washing-up you promised to help me with?'

But her question was drowned out by a bellow from the upstairs landing. 'Where have you been?' Hugo Lacey demanded, glaring down at them.

Marianne quailed. He'd found out about their visit to the camp.

'Sledging, Father,' Gerald answered. 'You said I could go, remember?'

'Yes, out enjoying yourself, when your grandmother has had a stroke and is at this moment probably dying.'

Chapter Nine

As the accusations of indifference and selfishness continued to rain down upon their heads, Marianne took hold of Gerald's hand and gave it a comforting squeeze. But he pulled away from her and ran up the stairs. Facing up to his father he said, 'I want to see Grandmama.'

'You can't. Don't you understand, you blockhead, she's ill.'

'I want to! I want to!' Gerald stamped his feet and started to sob in a childish, demanding way.

'You want a good tanning. Stop blubbing and go to your room.'

'No, I won't.' Gerald went to duck under his father's arm, but Hugo Lacey grabbed him by the neck and started to shake him as if he were no more than a stuffed doll. '*Behave!*' he roared.

'Don't, you'll kill him,' Marianne yelled, and raced up the stairs. The captain let go and stood staring at his hands, as if they belonged to someone else. Reaching out, Marianne put a protective arm round Gerald and gazed at her employer with contempt. Kids in Camberwell got slapped about a bit by their parents, but you didn't expect it from the upper classes. His life might be unravelling in front of his eyes, his mother dying, but his son was hardly to blame. Try telling him that, though, and as things stood, Marianne saw that it would be better if Gerald stayed out of his way. Giving the boy a gentle push, she said, 'Do as your father says, Master Gerald. You'll be able to see your grandmother as soon as she's a little better.'

'All right,' he mumbled, and without any more fuss he shuffled off along the landing to his bedroom.

Hugo Lacey waited until he'd closed the door; then, avoiding her eyes, he brushed past her. 'Go and sit with my mother, I must fetch the doctor. And pray that he's in.'

It's all right him giving orders, Marianne reflected, as she tiptoed into Mrs Lacey's room, but if she's already dead, what do I do then?

There was a small light by the bed, a clock that had escaped the auctioneer's hammer ticked loudly and the room had a stale, airless smell she would remember for the rest of her days. Marianne forced herself to approach the bed. Mrs Lacey was lying on her back; her eyes were closed, a trickle of saliva ran down the side of her mouth and her right arm lay stiff and awkward on the counterpane. But she was breathing. Poor thing. Marianne wiped the saliva away, pulled up a chair, sat down and took the thin hand in hers to reassure the woman that she wasn't alone. Occasionally she would make strange gurgling noises and Marianne, who knew about the death rattle, grew anxious. 'Please God, don't let her die just yet,' she prayed and, after what seemed an eternity but in reality was only half an hour, Marianne heard voices, then footsteps and sprang up to open the door.

'Thank you, Armstrong, Doctor Gibb will see to my mother now. I'll call you if I need you.'

It was at times like these that Marianne could see the point of a good stiff drink, instead she made do with the more well-tried formula; a cup of tea. She fed Boris and had just put him out when Hugo Lacey's head appeared round the door.

'Doctor Gibb has confirmed what I thought; my mother's had a stroke and he's gone back to his surgery to arrange to have her admitted to hospital. I shall go with her in the ambulance, but in the meantime could you pack a few things?'

Marianne stood up. 'Yes, of course. And I'm truly sorry about Mrs Lacey and I'll do whatever I can to help.'

'Keep an eye on Gerald for me. His tendency to hysteria is worrying. If it continues I shall have to have him looked at.'

'Looked at? Who by?'

'Why, a psychiatrist.'

Marianne was about to protest that Gerald's only problem was lack of affection, when the ambulance, its bell clanging, came hurtling up the drive. While Hugo Lacey went to let the ambulance men in, Marianne hurried upstairs to pack a bag for his mother, still thinking about what he'd said. There was definitely something unnatural about his coldness towards his son, she thought not for the first time, as she put a couple of nightgowns, a knitted bed-jacket, towel, soap and flannel into an overnight bag.

She was closing it when she heard her employer say, 'My mother is in here.' Two men followed him into the room and lifted Mrs Lacey on to a stretcher. Marianne was behind them as they carried her downstairs and she noticed Gerald's door open a fraction. She put a warning finger to her lips, but he didn't make a fuss and stood there quietly observing. He remained like that until the front door closed, then he ran to the landing window. Pressing his head against the glass, he said in a plaintive voice, 'Why does everyone leave me?'

Overwhelmed by his childish misery, Marianne went and gave him a consoling hug. 'Don't get upset, your grandmother will be taken good care of in hospital, and I'm sure you'll be able to go and visit her before long.' When there was no response, she went on, 'How'd you fancy a mince pie?'

He turned from the window, tiredly rubbed his eyes, then wiped his nose along the length of his sleeve. 'Actually, I am quite hungry.'

'There's that joint of cold pork in the larder. I could make some sandwiches.'

'Sounds scrumptious.'

She took his hand. 'Come on then.' As Nan used to say, there were occasions when a bit of spoiling did no harm, so Marianne plastered the bread with Renée's butter and added extravagant amounts of cold pork and stuffing. When they'd seen off the sandwiches and mince pies, Marianne thought to herself, well, it is Christmas, and opened a tin of pineapple.

'That was smashing,' said Gerald, lifting the plate and draining the last drop of juice into his mouth. As they sat there, warm and with full stomachs, it occurred to Marianne that, for the first time since she'd arrived, she was no longer hostage to Mrs Lacey's constantly ringing bell.

A week later they were into 1947, Mrs Lacey was still in hospital, 'with no change in her condition', and Gerald went back to school. Since no one else had bothered, at midnight Marianne opened the front door to let the New Year in, wished herself a prosperous one, (some hope) and went to bed comforted by the thought that she'd see Franz in the morning. But he didn't turn up, not on that day nor on the ones that followed. Neither Marianne nor Gerald voiced their fears, but they both knew there could only be one reason for Franz's absence: he'd been repatriated. But then Gerald came bouncing home one afternoon with some joyous news, Franz hadn't been sent back to Germany, but was working on a dairy farm on the other side of Stretton Magna.

For the first time for days, Marianne smiled.

'So can we go and see Laurel and Hardy at the village hall tonight?' Gerald asked.

'We certainly can.' The tyre on the bike was flat so they had to walk to the village, then they found themselves at the end of a long queue to buy tickets and when they did eventually get inside the hall, there wasn't a free seat. 'Looks like we're going to have to stand,' Marianne was saying, when Gerald nudged her. 'There's Franz waving to us.'

'Come, I have seats for you,' he called. Gerald grabbed Marianne's hand and dragged her down the aisle. But as they pushed their way along the row, Marianne heard some censorious tut-tutting from a couple of older women in the seats behind. Well, it'll give them something to talk about, she thought defiantly, smiled up at Franz and whispered, 'I've missed you.'

'And I've missed you, too, but I will come and see you soon,' Franz promised and, as the lights came down and the film began, he took her hand in his.

So far, though, Franz hadn't kept his promise. The days dragged on and the house, denuded of life, took on an even sadder aspect. With only the ghosts of her imagination to fill it, it took Marianne a while to see the benefits of having the place to herself, to realize that she was at no one's beck and call. She was free do as she pleased, read or lounge about as the mood took her.

But Marianne was unused to idleness; she was soon bored and looking for occupation. Then she hit upon an idea. She was never permitted to move anything in Mrs Lacey's room but now was the chance to give it a good clean-out, scour and scrub the smells away. Invigorated by the thought of honest labour, Marianne collected together mops, dusters and polish and rolled back her sleeves. Up went the windows, out went the fug, and in came some cold clean air. She stripped sheets and pillowcases off the bed, took them down to the wash-house and put them to boil in the copper. After adding Reckitt's blue to the final rinse, Marianne fed the bed linen through the mangle, hung it over the pulley to dry, then stood back to admire its dazzling whiteness.

A job well done, she decided, wiping the sweat from her brow, but what now? Well, that incoming tide of old newspapers needed tackling for a start. Marianne was tempted to use them for the fire but, fearful of the old lady's reaction when she found them gone, she bundled them into neat piles and pushed them against the wall so that she could start vacuuming. Why, Marianne wondered, as she dragged out a chest of drawers to vacuum behind, did Mrs Lacey hoard newspapers? Was it a sort of barricade against a hostile world? The vacuum cleaner sucked up great gobbets of dust and, almost, a square of paper. Marianne picked it up to take a closer look. Clothing coupons. Well, the old lady isn't going to need these where she is, Marianne reasoned, and was about to pocket them when Nan's voice ordered sternly, 'Put those back, at once!'

Flushing with guilt, Marianne shoved them under a glass candlestick and wiped her hands down her apron to purge herself of her small transgression. What had got into her? She'd never done anything like that in her life before.

Shaken by her lapse, Marianne gave the furniture a quick polish and shut the window. After she'd put the vacuum cleaner away, she glanced at the clock. A good hour before Gerald got home. She had a choice: she could do something boring like iron the sheets, or continue her investigation of the family's history. It didn't take a toss of a coin to decide and Marianne made her way to the attic with a sense of anticipation.

She'd ploughed her way through numerous albums, some interesting, some not, and today she came across pictures of Queen Victoria's Golden Jubilee, and later her funeral, which brought the albums into the present century.

There was little more of interest until she came to a wedding group. Marianne studied it closely. It was of Mrs Lacey, younger, and actually smiling, with a young man standing beside her wearing a more doubtful expression. They were surrounded by bridesmaids; at least eight Marianne counted, as well as page boys, and a couple who bore a strong resemblance to the bride. It was certainly a 'money no object' style of wedding and her parents would have been the ones coughing up, which might have accounted for their sour expressions.

Underneath someone had thoughtfully provided information. *The marriage of Hugo and Euphemia June 1910*. Funny, she'd never thought of Mrs Lacey having a Christian name.

A few pages on there was Euphemia again, holding a baby in her arms, but with her husband now in uniform. Marianne flicked over the page to see whether he'd survived the Great War. Yes, there he was standing beside a rather impressive car, a Daimler, she would swear to it. Gosh, that brought back the memories.

What a day that had been. It was easy to laugh now at Nan's exploits, but there'd been some hair-raising moments. It must have been over ten years ago, and yet she could remember clearly Nan standing by the window, drawing on a fag in a restless sort of way, then turning to her and saying, 'I'm fed up bein' cooped up here, get yer coat on, we're going out.'

'Where to Nan?'

'Wait and see,' she answered, stubbed out her cigarette in the ashtray and ran upstairs. When she came back down she was wearing a jaunty Robin Hood hat with a large feather curling up from the brim. Marianne couldn't remember seeing it before, although that wasn't unusual.

They caught the number twelve bus and went upstairs so that Nan could smoke and stayed on all the way to Oxford Street, getting off, eventually, opposite Selfridges.

A policeman was standing in the middle of the road directing the traffic. He held up his hand so that they could cross safely and Nan smiled at him and said, 'Thank you, officer.'

Selfridges was huge with fine window displays, but Nan hadn't come to window-shop. Thrusting a couple of toffees into her granddaughter's hand, she said, 'Now I won't be long, so wait here, don't move and don't talk to any strangers.'

'But where you goin', Nan?'

'Inside,' she replied and disappeared through the revolving doors.

Jostled by a continuous flow of shoppers and trying not to feel abandoned, Marianne chewed the toffees and studied the elegantly attired dummies in the window. Growing tired of this, she autographed the plate glass with her index finger, *Mary*, as she had been in those far off days; then she did a few spins in the revolving door. An irate customer eventually put a stop to this game, which was just as well because by now she felt a bit sick. 'Come on, Nan, where 'ave you got to?' Then a dreadful thought struck her. Supposing her nan had forgotten about her and gone off home? She could just see her, shoes already kicked off, feet up and enjoying a fag and a cuppa.

She tried to remember that she was a big girl now, nearly eight, and only babies cried, but her bottom lip quivered and a tear was about ready to slip down her cheek, when a large shiny automobile drew up and a chauffeur jumped out. He opened the car door and, with perfect timing, a young woman floated out of Selfridges, followed by a shop assistant with parcels up to his chin. Nan was just behind with a fox fur draped round her shoulders.

'Where did yo...?'

'Shut up,' Nan hissed, grabbed her hand and pulled her round to the far side of the car. They dispensed with the services of the policeman this time and plunged recklessly into the traffic. It was terrifying: buses, cars and drays bore down on them, but by the grace of God they made it across the road.

At full gallop Nan dived down a side-street dragging Marianne behind her. It wasn't until she complained that she had a stitch in her side that her grandmother stopped. Falling against a wall and looking all hot and bothered, she exclaimed, 'God me 'eart,' and fanned her face with a hankie.

'Did you buy that, Nan?' she'd asked, staring at the fox's squashed-up face, which was just level with her nose.

'Questions, questions. 'Course I did, duckie,' said Nan chirpily and adjusted her hat.

Her grandmother got her breath back and was ready to move on. After crossing a leafy square they came to some expensive-looking shops. 'Classy round here,' Nan observed as they paused to look in the window of a car showroom. 'Fancy a ride in one of those, sweetheart?' she asked, smiling down at her grand-daughter.

'Ooh yeah.'

'Which one?'

'That big one, like the lady had.'

'Right. Keep mum, follow me and I'll see what I can do.'

Adjusting the fox fur, Nan swayed into the showroom as to the manner born and, adopting a plummy accent, gave the salesman a load of guff about her husband, Lord somebody or other, promising to buy her a car for her birthday, and how she rather liked the look of the Daimler and could she have a run in it?

Before long an eager young man was driving them down The Mall. As they passed Buckingham Palace Marianne waved, just in case the King and Queen happened to be looking out of one of the windows. It was a beautiful car; the engine purred, and the upholstery was all leather, the young man informed them.

'Lovely shop, Harrods, always do my Christmas shopping there,' Nan said in passing as they drove down Knightsbridge. When they got back to the showroom, Nan told the salesman that the car was absolutely perfect for her and her husband would phone the following day. At the thought of a sale the young man got so excited he nearly tripped over himself opening the door for them.

Nan managed to keep a straight face as she walked away from the showroom, but as soon as they turned the corner, she burst out laughing. 'Folks are easily taken in, ain't they?'

Yes they were, by Nan at least. As a reward for being a good girl, her grandmother took her for tea at a posh café, where she had ice cream in a small silver dish and a slice of Fuller's walnut cake.

She never saw grandmother in that fox fur again, but a couple of months later she did notice Mrs Pym, who kept the sweet shop on the corner, trotting off to church wearing one that looked exactly like it.

Chapter Ten

Marianne closed the album and wiped away a nostalgic tear. After all these years it was still clear as yesterday: that fox fur draped across her Nan's shoulders, the ride in the Daimler. Her grandmother's outings might have been unconventional, but by golly she had a gift for making a small girl's life exciting. Sometimes, though, it was a bit like living on a fairground switchback, one minute your heart was in your boots, the next you were top of the world. It hadn't all been sweetness and light either, and out of the blue almighty rows could flare up between Nan and Renée about things she didn't understand. One fight in particular stuck in her memory because of its ferocity. She had been skipping along the pavement between her aunt and grandmother, listening to them sniping at each other over some chap by the name of Jonny Ellis when, without warning, it became a shouting match.

When she was at full throttle Renée had a voice on her that carried halfway to France, and that day she really let rip at her mother, there in the middle of the street with curious neighbours looking on. 'Why you can't let him at least speak to her, I don't know, it ain't natural.'

Like mother, like daughter. Nan had a tongue on her too, and she went for Renée like a crow at carrion. 'And what he did wasn't natural either, and he'll see 'er over my dead body!' It got personal after that and nasty, until eventually Renée screamed, 'Stop it!' shoved her fingers in her ears and rushed off down the street sobbing loudly.

'Look at her, the silly cow,' Nan sneered, then grabbed Marianne's hand and dragged her off to the nearest pub where, after handing her out a packet of Smith's crisps and a glass of lemonade, she left her to kick her heels and wonder who this Jonny fella was.

When her grandmother re-emerged at last, she gathered her up in her arms and breathed whisky fumes all over her. 'He won't get anywhere near you, my little pet,' she vowed, then took her to Jones & Higgins and bought her another new dress.

All those pretty dresses, cupboards-full. Marianne glanced down at her shabby skirt and scuffed working shoes, the clothes she put on in the morning and took off again at night, automatically, without really noticing them. Nan would probably disown me these days, she reflected, putting the album away and brushing the dust from her skirt.

The first time her grandmother came to visit her after she was evacuated, Miss Webb, fearful of letting her loose in wicked Leicester, had insisted on accompanying her to the station. Two platform tickets were an extravagance Miss Webb couldn't afford, so they waited for Nan in the booking hall.

She'd always loved her grandmother's sunshine-yellow hair, but as she tripped towards them in her chimney-stack heels and with a saucy pillbox hat perched on her head, her no-nonsense foster parent gave one of her sniffs, a sniff that said it all: Huh! Mutton dressed as lamb.

But she could also see her grandmother weighing up Miss Webb: the shabby coat, wispy grey bun, woollen stockings, and her loyalty underwent a tug-of-war. She had grown fond of her elderly carer and knew that she found life a struggle. In fact, she suspected that the money that came with her was the only reason

Miss Webb had agreed to take in an evacuee, because she was by nature solitary. Her way of speaking also suggested better times, and she was wise and she'd passed some of that wisdom on to Marianne.

After the two women had exchanged pleasantries, *nice for the time of year* and so on and so forth Miss Webb didn't hang around. She gave Marianne her return ticket, followed by instructions to Nan to be sure to put her on the right bus, after which she went off to do some shopping in the market.

Her grandmother waited until she was out of earshot, then asked, 'So how do you get on with that dowdy old spinster?'

'Fine, Nan,' Marianne had assured her, which was true, although she did find the country dull compared with London.

'Good, 'cos bombs or no bombs, I don't want you stopping if you're unhappy. Not that I think the war will last long,' she added. 'In the meantime, how d'you fancy going to see a film, then maybe have a plate of fish and chips in a nice café when we come out?'

With an irrepressible optimism, Nan made the same prediction about the course of the war on every visit. In fact they were almost the last words she ever spoke to her. 'The bombing raids 'ave stopped, duckie, we've got Jerry on the run and in a matter of months this war will be over, you mark my words, and we'll all be back together again, you, me and Renée, just like the old times.'

Of course she hadn't taken into account the doodlebugs, or the even more deadly V2 rockets, one of which would wipe out a whole terrace of houses and its inhabitants, including her beloved grandmother.

Marianne made an effort to pull herself together. A girl of her age should be looking forward to the future, not harking back all the time. Well, she knew what would banish the blues: some new clothes. Nan would approve of that. And the sales were on in

Leicester and she had some money saved. First thing tomorrow, she'd head off to town, splash out on the coat and boots she'd been promising herself, and maybe, if the money didn't run out, a skirt as well. But nothing fancy, tweed perhaps, hard-wearing and warm.

Marianne found the sketchbook on her next visit to the attic. It had an unremarkable beige cover and was tucked away in the side-pocket of the trunk and easy to miss. The photographs and the family tragedies had rather overwhelmed her and at first she was in two minds about looking at it.

But Barbara Lawrence Her Diary, printed across the cover, roused her curiosity and she sat down. With one ear cocked for the ravenous child who would shortly arrive home from school, she opened the diary. But there were no juicy confessions, just a few pencil drawings of the house and garden. On the next page there was a sketch of the greenhouse, looking considerably less dilapidated than it did now, and underneath the information that this was where Felix displayed his orchid collection. After this things began to buck up, for Barbara had very skilfully drawn the railway line, then under construction and which nowadays ran close to the POW huts where Franz lived. There were horses and carts, and navvies with their pickaxes and shovels hacking their way through solid rock. She had even sketched the bridge then in the process of being built.

However, what really interested Marianne were the barbed comments Barbara had written underneath her sketches relating to a certain young lady called Anna.

My cousin Anna came with me today when I went out with my sketch pad. Since she has never shown the slightest interest in my hobby, I wondered why and I soon found out. Here Barbara had sketched a well-set-up young man wearing a jaunty hat and smoking a clay pipe. *Anna's interest appears to lie with this navvy who goes by the by the name of Jack Ellis. He's handsome, if you like muscular men, and a cut above the other navvies because he's obviously had some sort of education. But he smiles too much and, as Mama says, the devil hides behinds a smiling face. I have a good sense of these things as well and it is my guess is that he's on the run from the law, as many of these men often are, although Anna insists that he's a Stone Mason and very skilled. People around here hate the navvies, with their drinking and thieving and the bare-knuckle fighting, but my cousin loves to show off, to be different and infuriate the villagers. She tosses her head at them and she has but one ambition, and that is to leave Stretton Magna. But not with a navvy, surely, to live in a hovel dug out of the ground. For our families are respectable and owners of several acres of good arable land. We'd turned for home when we noticed a horseman approaching and he raised his hat and stopped to speak to us. The gentleman introduced himself as Hugo Lacey who, we know, has returned home after living in London for several years. Of course he couldn't take his eyes off Anna, but she is quite indifferent to him, and complained, as he walked on, how he and his brother Julian were really horrible to her when she was a small girl and used to pull her plaits. We also decided between us that he has returned home because of the money. His father, the squire, known to be living in straitened circumstances, has become a rich man overnight. For after some skilful negotiations he has been well compensated by the railway company which is now running its track over his land. Papa and Uncle George are very angry about this decision, for it was their hope that the railway company would choose our land. But alas they didn't and we remain as poor as ever and Papa keeps telling me that I must make a good match.*

So that was where the Lacey money came from: the railways, thought Marianne and jumped when the doorbell clanged. Shoving the sketchbook out of sight she ran downstairs to let Gerald in, and promised herself that she'd be back in the attic the first chance she had.

It was clear to Marianne as soon as she woke the following morning that she wouldn't be going to Leicester for the foreseeable future. Hope Grange appeared to be floating on great drifting waves of snow, Boris's kennel had almost disappeared under a snowdrift and it took a good ten minutes to dig out a shivering, depressed-looking dog.

Only Gerald, delighted to be spared the agony of multiplication tables, welcomed the snow. Bouncing into the kitchen, he sat down at the table. 'Hurrah, no school.'

'And no milk delivery either,' Marianne retorted, her head half in the larder as she stared worriedly at their meagre rations.

'There's enough milk for breakfast, isn't there?'

'If you like powdered milk there is.'

'Don't worry, this'll be slush tomorrow.'

Marianne's head reappeared. 'Oh, so you can forecast the weather now?'

Gerald shrugged. 'Sort of. Anyway, what have we got?'

'There's some dried egg, half a loaf, porridge oats and a tin of Spam, otherwise the cupboard is like Old Mother Hubbard's, bare. We're low on coal, too, and if the logs run out ...' Marianne didn't finish. It would be nice to believe that Gerald's weather predictions were accurate, but there was no reason why this snow shouldn't carry on through January, February and March. In fact they could become so cut off, people would forget they existed until one spring day someone would take a walk up here and find nothing but two frozen corpses and a dead dog.

'Don't worry, Armstrong, we've got plenty of trees and Franz will always come and cut another one down for us,' said Gerald with childish optimism.

Yes, he was right and it was that silly imagination of hers working overtime. Franz wouldn't leave them to freeze to death and, cold-hearted as he was, neither would Hugo Lacey.

'And you've got me,' he reminded her.

Turning her back to hide her smile, Marianne measured the porridge oats into a saucepan, added salt and water and stirred. When the porridge was cooked, she poured it into two plates and they ate it with the reconstituted milk and a sprinkling of sugar.

'Warmed the cockles of me heart, that did,' said Marianne, when she'd scooped up the last spoonful.

Gerald wrinkled his nose. 'Glad you liked it.'

'Worse where there's none,' Marianne replied tartly, cut two slices of bread, and spread them with margarine and a smear of jam. Gerald ate his slowly, dabbing his index finger around the plate to gather up every last crumb.

'Is that all?'

''Fraid so.' Marianne got up from the table. 'I'm going upstairs to have a listen on your grandmother's wireless. There might be a weather forecast.'

'What shall I do?'

'Well, you could get on with some school work, a few sums, or maybe write an essay.'

'That's boring.'

'Life *is* boring: cooking, cleaning is boring. Read a book then.'

'I think I'll play with Boris.'

'Please yourself.' It was hard enough trying to keep this dilapidated house functioning and she had no intention of adding Gerald's education to her list of tasks.

Marianne switched on the radio and waited for the announcer's voice, but when it came it was barely audible. 'The blinking accumulator's flat again,' she muttered angrily. Out of sheer frustration she gave the radio a shake, pressed her ear against the fretwork and caught something about a dock strike and food being held up. Just what the country needs, she thought bitterly, and went back downstairs.

But Gerald was right about the weather and the following day it thawed enough to pack him off to school and for Marianne to walk into the village against a wind that flayed her skin. She then stood in the slush outside the butcher's, resigning herself to chilblains, unless she could get into Leicester to buy those fur-lined boots she'd promised herself. At last it was her turn to be served and her waiting was rewarded with two sausages, a couple of pigs' kidneys and four rashers of bacon.

'How's Mrs, Lacey then?' Mr Veal asked as he wrapped her purchases.

'About the same.'

'I hear Gerald hasn't bin to see her yet.'

'His father's taking him Saturday.' He was doing nothing of the sort, but it irritated her the way Mr Veal felt he was entitled to know everyone's business. However, she was careful to keep her opinion to herself, for if the butcher took against her, choicer cuts could disappear under the counter.

Marianne paid him, wished him good day, then walked across to Miss Hardcastle's. Here there was another queue of cold, resentful housewives. 'That old biddy in there keeps us waiting deliberately,' said one.

'And how much longer is Attlee going to keep us on ration books and shortages, that's what I'd like to know. The war's over, for God's sake,' complained another.

'Do you realize it's freezing out there?' said a woman when at last they were packed inside.

Miss Hardcastle bristled. 'I'm hardly responsible for the weather. Now, who's first?'

'Me,' a woman piped up. 'Can I have a dozen candles please?'

'No candles.'

'No candles?' Marianne queried; she was standing right behind the other shopper. 'Are you sure?'

'Quite sure.'

'What about oranges?'

'Yeah, come on, cough up,' the women behind her chorused.

'Oranges?' Miss Hardcastle repeated in tones of disbelief. 'Certainly not.'

'That's funny, I read in the *Mercury* that a large consignment of oranges has arrived and they're to be distributed to all children under eighteen.'

'Oh, you don't want to believe everything you read in the papers.'

Fed up, cold and tired of having to beg for every morsel of food, Marianne's temper snapped. 'It's like the bananas we never get and the candles you've run out of, isn't it?'

'I don't know what you're talking about.'

'Ever heard of the black market?'

'How dare you imply such a thing!'

'I more than imply, Miss Hardcastle; in fact I'm going to report you to the Ministry of Food.'

With a theatrical toss of her head, Marianne swept out, helped on her way by cheers from the other women.

'Here, you wait a minute,' Miss Hardcastle called.

Marianne paused with her hand on the door handle. 'Are you talking to me?' Then, as she had known would happen, a bundle of candles appeared from under the counter, then an orange and something she hadn't seen for a long time, a banana.

'That's the last,' announced the shopkeeper.

'I'm sure it's not,' Marianne replied, as she put the booty in her shopping bag and paid. 'Unless you want the police investigating I'm sure you'll be able to oblige these other ladies, Miss Hardcastle.'

'Yeah, hand over that stuff yer hoarding.' The women pushed against the counter in a threatening manner and the last sight Marianne had of the shopkeeper was of her hurriedly dishing out candles and oranges to her customers. An unfamiliar sense of power kept her going, and she hurried home thinking: it just shows what you can achieve if you're prepared to stick your neck out and stand up for your rights. It was a lesson, Marianne decided, she would try to remember.

The following evening Hugo Lacey rushed into the kitchen where they were having supper, and stood in front of Gerald. 'Get your coat on, I'm taking you to see your grandmother.'

As they drove off, Marianne wondered what the hurry was because, in spite of Gerald continually pleading to be taken to visit his grandma, until now his father had fobbed him off with various excuses, such as that his mother didn't feel up to it, or it wasn't convenient, he hadn't the time and so on and so forth.

When it reached midnight and they hadn't returned, Marianne began to suspect the worst. And she was right. She heard the car and prepared herself. Gerald came in sobbing and Hugo Lacey was making repeated use of a hip flask.

He took a swig, turned away, cleared his throat and said, 'My mother passed away peacefully at eleven o'clock this evening.'

'Oh, I am sorry, Captain Lacey.'

'Yes ... well ... she had a weak heart and I was warned that she might not recover. I shall go to my room now. Tomorrow I will have to make arrangements for the funeral.'

'Can I bring you something up?'

'No, thank you.'

Marianne locked the doors and dragged herself tiredly up the stairs. There'd been no love lost between her and Mrs Lacey, but she still felt a certain sadness, if only because it had seemed such an unfulfilled life. Ridiculously, she also thought of the beautifully clean bedroom she would never see. Before going on up to her own room, Marianne paused, then went and knocked on Gerald's bedroom door. When there was no reply, she opened it a fraction. He was lying on the bed fully clothed and fast asleep. Marianne covered him with blankets and thought, poor little blighter, who's he got to love him now?

The funeral cortège was meagre to say the least of it. No relatives – had they not been invited or weren't there any? However, curtains were drawn across windows in the village, men doffed their caps and Mr Veal was there in the congregation, and Miss Hardcastle, the doctor and his wife and a sprinkling of villagers who might have worked for the family in the past were there as a mark of respect.

Marianne found her thoughts becoming disjointed; this funeral became muddled with that other dreadful day: the telegram, the dazed journey from Leicester, the drive through the ruined London streets to Camberwell, the funeral service. That church had been full, spilling over with grief and a raging anger at the loss of loved ones. So different, Marianne thought, gazing about her, from the polite, distant respect being paid to Mrs Lacey.

The congregation was rising. '*I am the resurrection and the life ... We brought nothing into this world ...*' the vicar intoned as he preceded the pallbearers into the church. Gerald, pale, eyes down, hands crossed in front of him, walked beside his father, who stared stiffly ahead. The coffin was placed on the bier and Marianne learnt more about Mrs Lacey during the short service than she had in all the weeks she'd looked after her. The vicar spoke of her love for her son and her grandson, and for her husband and the sadness of his early death; of her exceptional singing voice, her deep faith and love of travel and hunting. Well, it was a comfort to know that her life hadn't been as pointless as she'd imagined, Marianne reflected as she looked for her place in the hymn book. '*When our heads are bow'd with woe,*' had been one of the chosen hymns on that other occasion in Camberwell as well, and as she sang Marianne's voice cracked with emotion. She was grateful for the prayer that followed, because it gave her space to compose herself.

There were a couple more hymns, then they trooped out to the churchyard. In front of her Marianne could see Gerald, his small face puckered with misery and trying hard not to cry. A deep hole had been pickaxed out of the frozen earth and the coffin was lowered into it. '*Earth to earth, ashes to ashes, dust to dust.*' Hugo Lacey picked up a handful of earth and, indicating to Gerald that he should follow suit, he sprinkled it on to the coffin. Gerald did as he was bid, his shoulders heaving convulsively.

'*Lord, have mercy upon us. Christ, have mercy upon us. Lord, have mercy upon us.*' As the interment came to its conclusion Marianne turned and walked away. Her eyes were brimming with tears, not for Mrs Lacey, whose funeral this was, but for her grandma and all the murdered children in that street with whom she'd once played and squabbled.

The next time Marianne ventured up to Mrs Lacey's bedroom it was to find that it had been stripped: bed, chest of drawers, chair, carpets, all gone, only the bundles of newspapers remained. 'They've even taken the wireless,' Marianne grumbled to Boris, who'd trundled up after her. It took a fearfully cold heart to obliterate all memories of a mother so soon after her death, but Hugo Lacey had done it, and all for a few pounds in his pocket. Maybe she'd come home one day and find her own bed gone, swapped for a bottle of whisky.

The wireless would have been company and the loss of it rankled. She'd planned to have the accumulator recharged and keep it the kitchen, where she could listen to the dance bands and comedy shows like ITMA and Variety Bandbox. More important, it would have kept her up to date on the weather, because it was coming to dominate her life and just when Marianne thought it couldn't get any worse, it did.

Chapter Eleven

By late January the whole country was snowbound. Twenty-foot-high drifts made roads impassable, branch lines to collieries were blocked, potato clamps frozen. Then they started getting power cuts, anything from one hour to five. Marianne spent her waking hours tussling with the everyday problems of producing meals and trying to keep the house minimally warm and this monotonous daily grind really got her down, so that she became so low-spirited and snappy, Gerald and Boris found it best to keep out of her way. It didn't help that she also began to fear that Franz had already grown tired of her. She'd never had a boyfriend, had never been in love before, so all she knew about men was what she read in books. In books they could be fickle, so when Franz said he loved her maybe he didn't mean it. Until now she had believed him totally, which was perhaps a bit naïve and trusting, for surely, if he did love her, he would move heaven and earth to see her.

To add to her woes, she was down to her last half-crown and Hugo Lacey hadn't been near the place for two weeks. If they weren't to starve, pretty soon she'd have to dip into her savings, money she'd been putting aside for the new clothes she craved, or in case Renée let her down. Because Marianne was clear in her mind on one point: she was giving her aunt until March, then it was goodbye to this place – and Gerald, she thought, with a guilty glance in his direction.

He was crouched in front of the fire in his winceyette pyjamas. Until a few minutes ago they'd been playing snap, but he was such a bad loser that in the end Marianne lost patience with him and slapped down her cards.

'Right, I'm not playing any more,' she announced firmly. This brought on a real sulk and since she didn't want it to go on all evening, she said, as a peace-offering, 'Like some cocoa?'

He nodded.

'Cat got your tongue?'

He stuck it out at her.

'You do try my patience. Yes or no?'

'Yes. Please,' Gerald remembered in time.

Marianne made the cocoa, found a couple of rich tea biscuits, passed one over to Gerald and sat back with a sigh. Sitting round the fire like this sipping cocoa brought back memories. 'D'you know, when I was a kid, in winter Nan used to turn out the lights and we'd sit round the fire singing along with the "Ovaltinies" on Radio Luxembourg. Would you like me to sing to you?'

'No thanks. Armstrong, why do you only ever talk about your nan, never your mother?' Gerald enquired, spooning sugar from the bottom of the mug. 'Have you got one?'

'Everyone has a mother, we wouldn't be here otherwise, but mine died when I was born. Barely sixteen she was and little more than a child herself.' She could still remember the break in her Nan's voice when she related the story. 'It was a terrible labour, too much for her small body and she just gave up the ghost and died. I'll never get over it, not if I live to be a hundred.'

But Gerald was too young to be burdened with these grisly details, although he was looking interested.

'So where's your father?' he asked.

Now this was wading in muddy waters. 'He's dead too.' Well, he might be and Nan's comments, when she asked about him, had been unrepeatable in polite society. *I don't ever want to hear the* word *'father' pass your lips in this house, do I make myself clear? He dishonours the name, but if I ever get my hands on the bastard I'll throttle him*, she'd promised and that had been that. All Marianne knew about her father was that he'd done something unforgivable in her grandmother's eyes.

'So you're an orphan?' said Gerald.

'More or less.'

Gerald wiped away the small moustache of cocoa that had formed on his upper lip and looked thoughtful. 'My mother ... she ...' He was forcing himself to speak.

Marianne held her breath. *Don't say a word, wait for it.*

'... she ... she ...' he stumbled, and at that critical moment, when she might have discovered Felicity's whereabouts, they were plunged into darkness.

'Damn and blast, another power cut,' Marianne cursed. She put a taper to the fire and lit a candle.

Evidently feeling he'd said too much, Gerald stood up and put his mug on the table. 'I'm going to bed. Will you to come up with me?'

'Of course.' Although he was too proud to admit it, she sensed he was nervous of the dark, and who wouldn't be in this great crumbling pile? Marianne pressed one candle into the wine bottle she'd kept, another into an old-fashioned chamber-stick, and led the way up the stairs. The candlelight threw their shadows against the wall and turned them into hunched monsters. Clutching her skirt, Gerald asked, 'Do you believe in ghosts?'

'Of course not,' Marianne lied, because hadn't she heard them, seen them in this very house?

'Will you look under the bed?'

'If you wish.' Marianne swept the candlelight around the room, peered under the bed, behind the door and, on his insistence, inside the wardrobe. 'What did I say, nothing there. Now into bed.'

'I shall mention it to God when I say my prayers, ask him to keep them away,' he replied, apparently not convinced by her reassurances.

'I'm sure he'll oblige.'

'Will you kiss me good night, Armstrong?' he asked, as she tucked him in.

'If you call me Marianne I will.'

'Will you kiss me goodnight, Marianne? Please.'

Marianne laughed. This was more like the old Gerald. 'Of course.' She leaned over and as she pressed her lips against his cheek, his arms came up around her neck, then with a contented sigh, he turned over on his side and closed his eyes. 'G'night Marianne.'

'Goodnight, sleep tight, don't let the bugs bite.' Closing the door Marianne thought, a right pair we are, swilled about by the tide, part of the flotsam and jetsam of life.

'No excuses now, Captain Lacey, get yourself up here and pay me,' Marianne ordered, as she watched the snowplough come through, followed by the POW lorry with men and shovels to clear the drive.

'Franz is here! Franz is here!' Gerald yelled and a moment later there he was, standing in the kitchen, the man she thought had abandoned her.

'Hello.' His smile was sweet, tender.

'Hello,' Marianne answered shyly, then Franz opened his arms. Although she longed to fly into them she didn't dare and Gerald rushed to fill her place. 'I love you,' Franz mouthed over Gerald's head and immediately everything was all right.

'And I love you,' she murmured, touching him lightly as they stood smiling at each other.

'But how are you both?'

'Cold and a bit hungry and we've spent a lot of time in the dark.'

The lorry horn sounded and Franz backed out of the door. 'I must go now. We have many, many people to dig out.'

'But you will come back, won't you, Franz?' Gerald demanded, tugging on the sleeve of his overcoat.

'Yes, tomorrow if I can.'

And he did, bringing with him a bag of potatoes, two quarts of milk and feed for the chickens.

Marianne fell upon the gifts. 'Bless you, Franz. We'll make a meal of these potatoes tonight.'

'Mr Thornton, the farmer, he is a nice man and he gave them to me, and the milk. I can milk a cow now,' he added proudly. 'And he says I can stay and chop wood for you.'

'But when are you going to come back and work for us?' asked Gerald.

Franz shrugged. 'I do not know. There is much work to do at the farm, but not here, for the ground it is frozen hard and covered in snow and I cannot dig it. But the cows, they need looking after. I like cows,' he added, 'they are nice.'

'What, nicer than us?'

Franz laughed. 'No, but sometimes they are naughty like you.'

'In what way?'

'They kick the milk pail over. But now I will go and saw up many logs for you and I will come back every week, I promise.'

'I'll come and help you,' said Gerald and off the two of them went, out into the bitter cold, and gradually the woodpile grew until it was level with the sill. On and on Franz and Gerald worked until it was almost dark and eventually Marianne had to go and call them in.

She sniffed the resinous air. Even without a coal delivery there were enough logs to keep them going for several days. And the newspapers Mrs Lacey had hoarded were proving to be a useful standby. As she approached, Gerald emerged from the stables holding aloft a pair of ice skates.

'Look what I found.' He sat down, pulled off his wellington boots and tried them on. 'See, they fit. I expect they were my father's. I'm going to have a skate on the pond.'

He went to move off but Marianne grabbed him. 'Oh no, you aren't. It's almost dark, Franz has worked hard all afternoon and he deserves a cup of tea and a piece of toast.'

'I like the sound of that,' said Franz, and with arms linked, the three of them walked back to the house.

Gerald was so possessive, it was hard for them to spend a minute alone, but when Franz was about to leave, Marianne sent Gerald upstairs on some pretext and they fell into each other's arms.

'I do love you so much, and I think of you every minute, and one day we will marry,' Franz murmured and covered her face with kisses.

'If only we could find somewhere to meet,' Marianne whispered, then that was it, because Gerald came clattering down the stairs and they jumped guiltily apart.

The next day Hugo Lacey found time for a brief visit. 'Sorry to neglect you for so long, but I've finally managed to get hold of some wheel-chains. As long as we don't get any more of these gigantic snowdrifts I should be home regularly. You appear to have survived quite well, though,' he said, glancing at the pile of logs rising above the kitchen windowsill. 'And there was I worrying about you.'

'You were right to be worried, there hasn't been a coal delivery for ages and we were almost out of fuel. Franz worked all day yesterday sawing up those logs, and on top of that I'm down to my last shilling.'

'So, even a German has his uses.' He reached into his pocket and drew out a wallet. 'Your wages and the housekeeping money.' He placed several notes on the table. Marianne picked them up and counted them. 'I'm ten shillings short.'

He shot her a furious glance, and banged another note on the table. 'Where is Gerald?'

'Outside making a snowman.'

'Go and tell him I wish to speak to him, please. I'll be in my office.'

Wondering what it was he had to say to his son, Marianne went in search of Gerald. Hugo Lacey never willingly engaged him in conversation, so it would have to be important. It might also have some bearing on her own future.

She found the completed snowman but no Gerald and no Boris. Imagining his father in his office striding impatiently up and down, she cupped her hands and called, 'Gerald, where are you? Your father is here and wants a word with you.'

No response. She poked her head in the stables. Empty. Marianne was about to move on when behind her, a voice demanded, 'Haven't you found him yet?'

What a stupid question, obviously I haven't. 'He'll be around somewhere.'

'Wretched boy. I have to be away, and as usual, he's being a pest.' Hugo Lacey pulled back his cuff and checked his watch. 'Gerald, stop this tomfoolery and tell us where you are,' he shouted.

That got a response. 'I'm here, Father, skating, on the lake.'

'What's he talking about? The child can't skate.'

They looked at each other then began to run. Gerald, arms stretched wide to balance himself, was wobbling around the edge of the lake, while Boris ran up and down whimpering in an agitated manner.

The muscles in his face working, his father shouted, 'Gerald, get off the ice, this minute!'

In an act of sheer bravado, Gerald ignored his father and made off towards the middle of the lake. Beside her, Marianne felt Hugo Lacey tense. Neither spoke, both of them held their breath. The ice might just hold.

When he was as far from safety as it was possible to be, Gerald turned, grinning with pride and eager to impress his father. 'See, I've done it, Father.' As he spoke, there was a crack like a pistol shot, the ice shattered and with a look of surprise and terror on his small face, Gerald slid into the freezing water.

'Oh, my God!' Without thinking, Marianne ran on to the ice, but Hugo Lacey grabbed and pulled her back.

'Don't be such an idiot.'

Gerald surfaced, scrabbling to hold on to ice that was collapsing around him. 'Let me go, he's drowning!' Marianne screamed and tried to pull away from Hugo.

'You'd be more help if you stopped panicking,' Hugo snapped. 'It won't take your weight as well, so stay where you are,' he ordered. He lowered himself on to the ice and slithered on his belly towards the centre, reaching Gerald as he resurfaced, spluttering and covered in rank weeds. 'Grab my hand,' his father shouted, but he was too far away and Gerald went under again.

Hugo edged closer to the jagged edges of the broken ice and Marianne put her hand to her mouth. Oh God, he'll be in the water himself in a second. In her distress, it was a moment before she noticed that Boris was gingerly making his way across the ice. Holding her breath, Marianne watched. He'd never make it. But she'd underestimated the dog, and somehow Boris managed to reach the drowning child. As he came up for the third time he locked his teeth over his coat collar and dragged him clear of the putrid water.

Not sure that her heart could cope with any more drama, Marianne turned away and closed her eyes. She didn't open them again until she was certain Gerald, Boris and Hugo were all safely on dry land. Gerald was lying on the snow, blue-lipped and unconscious and covered in green slime. Apart from an unusual pallor, Hugo showed no emotion, but he got to work immediately on Gerald, clearing his mouth of debris, then turning him on to his stomach and pressing down on his lungs until a great jet of slime spurted out his mouth. 'He's breathing,' he said tersely. He removed his greatcoat, wrapped his son in it and hurried back to the house. Meanwhile Boris, shivering and ignored, followed behind.

It wasn't until they reached the back door that Marianne, to her great shame, realized that she'd been so taken up with Gerald's fate that she had forgotten it was Boris who'd saved him. She bent and put her arms round his neck and kissed him. 'You were a good, brave dog, Boris, and you deserve a medal for saving that young man's life,' she told him. Boris wagged his tail and gave her a look that said, 'Yes, I know I do.'

In the kitchen Hugo Lacey laid his son down in front of the fire. 'Get blankets,' he ordered, and by the time Marianne returned he'd removed the soaking clothes and was rubbing Gerald's body vigorously.

'It's to get the blood circulating,' he explained and stood up. 'Can you take over? I must go and fetch the doctor.'

Marianne piled on the blankets but as soon as she heard Hugo drive off, she let Boris in. Immediately the dog lumbered over to Gerald and started licking his face. There was no response to start with but then Gerald's lids began to flicker, his eyes opened and when he saw Boris he gave a weak smile. By the time his father returned with Doctor Gibb, Gerald was conscious, but floppy and not sure where he was.

'Light a fire in the bedroom, I'll examine him up there.' The doctor's tone to Marianne was precise, clipped, and as soon as she'd got the fire going her employer brought Gerald upstairs and laid him on the bed. Doctor Gibb took some time examining Gerald and his expression was solemn when removed his stethoscope. 'Well, he's lucky to be alive, but I'm not going to beat about the bush, Hugo; the next few days are going to be critical. Pneumonia could develop, so he needs constant care.'

'But I must get back.'

'Someone will have to sit with him tonight, Hugo.' The doctor's voice was polite but firm.

'All right, I'll stay.' The captain spoke with the air of a man making a great sacrifice.

Marianne herself spent a restless night and once she crept down to Gerald's room to check that his father was still with him. He was, but asleep and the fire was low. Neither of them stirred as she added more logs, but when she went in again the following morning the fire was out and Gerald was on his own. But Marianne could hear movement downstairs and when she went into the kitchen, Hugo Lacey was there, dressed in his uniform and drinking a cup of tea.

'Gerald had a good night and I have a meeting I can't miss, but I'll pop back in a day or two to check.' He gulped down his tea, pushed his arms into his greatcoat and marched to the door.

But Marianne went after him. Gerald was his son and he wasn't leaving her with all the responsibility. 'Is there any way I can get in touch with you, Captain Lacey?'

'Doctor Gibb has my phone number. Don't worry, Armstrong, my son comes from healthy stock, and he'll be back on his feet in a couple of days. And when he is I'll have a word to say to him about putting me to all this inconvenience.' Adjusting his cap in the hall mirror and leaving Marianne to close the door, he got into his car.

'You hard-hearted monster,' Marianne mouthed to the departing vehicle, turned and found Gerald crouched halfway down the stairs.

'Get back into bed immediately,' she ordered.

'I thought my father was going to stay with me,' he said tearfully as Marianne clamped the blankets firmly around him.

'He would have if he could, but he's on important work and the army needs him. He'll be back in a day or two,' Marianne explained and wondered why she was bothering to protect the man.

'And he'll come and sit with me?'

'Of course. But right now I'm going to light the fire again, make you some tea and toast. Then, if I bring Boris up here to keep you company, do you think you'll be all right on your own for a short while? There's no telling what the weather will do and I need to go to the shops.'

Gerald raised his head a little. 'Boris saved my life, didn't he?'

'Yes, and you're very lucky to be here, because what you did yesterday was extremely foolish,' said Marianne sternly.

'I thought it would make my father proud of me.' Gerald plucked the sheets. 'Because, you see, I don't think he loves me very much.'

'Whereever did you get that silly notion from? Of course he loves you, and so does Boris and so do I.'

'Not when I'm being beastly you don't.'

She put her arm around him and kissed the top of his head. 'We all behave badly at times and your behaviour is improving,' Marianne assured him, but he didn't hear her because he had fallen asleep.

She relit the fire, woke Gerald and gave him his breakfast, which he hardly touched, then took Boris up. The reunion between child and dog was ecstatic and Marianne set off for the village with an easy mind.

She purchased the week's rations at Miss Hardcastle's to a chilly silence and at Mr Veal's to the usual questions. 'My lad tells me that Gerald in't in school. All right, is 'e?'

'No, he's in bed, doctor's orders. He went skating on the lake and fell in.'

'My Lord, what was the foolish boy up to? I heard just the other day that a couple of girls drowned playing on the ice on the canal. It can happen in a flash.'

'If it hadn't been for Boris, Gerald would have drowned.'

Mr Veal added a bone to the parcel. 'A reward for a brave dog. So how is the lad now?'

'Recovering slowly.'

'Pa with him?'

'No, the captain had to get back to his ... wherever it is he goes.'

'He's a paper-pusher in some army camp out Lincoln way.'

'Is that so?' He'd always given the impression that he was engaged in top secret work, hence his frequent absences. 'He'll be home at the weekend, though; he's promised.'

'Depends on the weather. Forecast in't good.' Marianne paid the butcher and as he handed her her purchases, he leaned over the counter and said in a confidential tone, 'I've put in a couple of pigs' trotters for you.'

Marianne thanked him somewhat insincerely, although she supposed they were an improvement on last week's grey slab of tripe. Pigs' trotters had been one of her grandmother's favourite dishes, but she couldn't stand the gristly things; she knew she would be hard put to make them tasty and have to be damned hungry to eat them.

However, the butcher had thoughtfully wrapped them in a page of yesterday's *Leicester Mercury* and when she got home Marianne spread it out on the kitchen table. Although there were smears of blood on it, it was readable and as usual, the paper was full of bossy government directives. *Plan your cooking to save fuel. Do not heat more water than you need.* On and on it went. Marianne wondered who thought up all these depressing slogans. A man, she bet, some little twerp sitting at his desk in Whitehall, with nothing better to do than make life even more difficult for the housewife. Marianne gave an irritated huff and turned over the page. A photograph of hundreds of people queuing for coke at the gasworks in Leicester with handcarts and prams was spread right across the page. Many of them had been standing there since three in the morning, according to the caption, and several had fainted with the cold.

Poor devils. As if the British hadn't suffered enough during six years of war, now we're having to endure the worst winter in living memory. But then sorrows never came singly. Brooding on this, Marianne went and stacked away the food in the larder.

When she'd finished she went to check on Gerald. He was asleep and Boris lay by his bed snoring, although he did open one eye. 'Good boy,' she said, 'you've looked after him.' In defiance of the Whitehall directive Marianne added more logs to the fire, then went back down to the kitchen to see if she could find a recipe for pig's trotters.

Because he knew he'd been stupidly reckless Gerald never again referred to the accident and neither did Marianne. She'd already said her piece and Gerald still had to face his father, who would have plenty to say on the subject, accompanied, no doubt, by some form of chastisement.

In spite of his father's wrath hanging over him, Gerald continued to make good progress. His appetite improved, and as he grew stronger he began demanding to be allowed downstairs. Marianne, however, was adamant; he would stay in bed until his father came home.

'You must read to me, then,' Gerald ordered and gradually Marianne worked her way through the *William* books, Enid Blyton's *Famous Five* and Kipling's *Just So Stories*. There was one book, though, which he begged her to read time and again, a rather tedious tale about a family, three unbelievably well-behaved children, a paragon of a mother who never raised her voice, and a father who went off to work each morning in a bowler hat and returned promptly at 5.30 stone-cold sober. The book was illustrated and whenever they came to a picture of the saintly mother, Gerald would stare at her hard and long as if trying to conjure up his own mother. In the end Marianne grew so irritated with the honey-coated characters that she tried to avoid reading it. Why, she wondered, did nobody write the truth about family life, about disappearing mothers, drunken fathers and badly behaved children.

On the Saturday morning, when Marianne took Gerald up his breakfast he refused it and turned to face the wall. Thinking his behaviour might be due to his father's imminent homecoming and fear of punishment, Marianne leaned over him.

'Hey, what's up, she asked.

'My chest and my head hurt.'

'Badly?'

'Quite badly.'

Marianne took his temperature, it was touching 100°, she felt his forehead, it was burning. And he'd been doing so well, too. Thankful that she'd soon be able to hand the responsibility over to her employer, she sat with Gerald all morning, listening to his irregular breathing and taking his temperature every couple of hours. She tried not to panic as it continued to rise, but wished his father would hurry. Thinking she heard a car, Marianne went to the front window and found an impenetrable freezing fog pushing against the panes. Out on the flat lands of Lincolnshire it would be doubly bad. Even with the best intentions, she knew Hugo Lacey wouldn't get here today.

Gerald needed the doctor, but Marianne had a superstitious fear of leaving him. She knew it was a chance she had to take, though. 'I'm going to fetch Doctor Gibb, but I promise I won't be long,' she whispered in Gerald's ear, then called Boris to sit with him.

Franz had mended her flat tyre, but outside the fog was thick and played havoc with her sense of direction. Several times Marianne almost tumbled in a ditch, and once she found herself tangling with a hedge. The silence was eery, and of course the doctor's house had to be on the far side of the village.

His wife answered the door, and didn't look too pleased to find that her husband, who'd settled down to play ludo with his children, had a customer on a Saturday.

But Marianne was too desperate to be intimidated by her frosty manner. 'I work at Hope Grange,' she explained. 'Doctor Gibb came to see Gerald when he fell in the lake and he told us to watch for any change. Well his temperature's over a hundred and rising, he's very feverish, his father hasn't come home, and I don't know what to do so please, please you've got to let him come,' she pleaded in a tearful voice.

'Step inside a moment, I'll speak to my husband,' said Mrs Gibb. She disappeared into the back of the house while a cat sat at the bottom of the stairs and stared at Marianne with glassy disdain.

Doctor Gibb appeared a few minutes later, carrying his black bag. 'How did you get here?' he asked.

'On my bike.'

'You can fetch your bike later and come with me in the car and hope we don't meet any traffic.'

'How are you feeling, old chap?' Doctor Gibb asked as he felt Gerald's pulse.

'Ill,' Gerald answered faintly.

'Don't worry, we'll soon have you better,' said the doctor and turned to Marianne. 'Can you sit him up please?' he said, and put the stethoscope in his ears. He gave Gerald a thorough examination and when he'd finished he snapped shut his black bag and said to Marianne, 'We'll talk downstairs.'

'It's what I feared, pneumonia.'

'That's serious isn't it?'

'It is and we need to get him to hospital as quickly as possible.'

Doctor Gibb looked about him then gave a vexed sigh. 'Why on earth hasn't Hugo got a phone?'

Marianne didn't trouble to answer. Like everyone else in the village, he knew why: because the family was on its uppers.

'I'll have to go home and phone the hospital, but with this weather ...' he peered into the gloom ... 'it might be hours before the ambulance gets here.'

Marianne grabbed the doctor's arm. 'It could be too late by then. Can't you take him to the hospital in your car?'

Doctor Gibb looked taken aback at her suggestion. 'This weather, it's so unpredictable. If I had an accident we could both end up dead.'

'Please ...' she begged.

'All right.' The doctor ran up the stairs and bundled Gerald up in a blanket. 'Come on, old chap, I'm taking you to hospital.'

But it was obvious Gerald wasn't aware of much. His head lolled, his breathing was harsh and his skin was dry and burning.

Doctor Gibb laid him on the back seat, then came and patted Marianne's hand. 'Try not to worry, young lady, we have miracle drugs like penicillin now that cure almost everything. You'll have him home in no time.'

'You'll ring Captain Lacey and tell him Gerald's gone into hospital, won't you, Doctor?'

'I will.'

Marianne watched the car slide away into the fog, then went inside and barred the back and front doors. She sat down at the kitchen table, cupped her chin in her hands and thought: this house has a curse on it, and here's me all alone in it with just Boris, the ghosts, two guttering candles and this everlasting winter.

Chapter Twelve

Captive in the dark empty house, Marianne sat and thought: Nan gone, Mrs Lacey gone and now Gerald. The doctor talked blithely of cure-all drugs but she knew he wasn't coming back. She sort of mislaid people, like this good-for-nothing father of hers, recorded as 'Unknown' on her birth certificate and who, as her grandmother never missed a chance to tell her, had been responsible for her mother's death. In fact his rottenness had been fed into her all her life, and it so coloured her opinion of him that Marianne could still remember her dismay when, during a biology lesson at school, she'd learnt that as well as inheriting its parents' looks, a child also inherited their character, the bad along with the good. So distressed was she at the thought of growing up like her dad that Marianne's concentration flew out of the window and the morning ended with the teacher whacking her across her knuckles with a ruler for not paying attention.

That was enough and at dinner time she ran home in tears and sobbed her story out to her Nan.

'Fancy filling yer head with such rubbish. I've a good mind to take you away from that school.' Nan dragged angrily on her cigarette, then threw it in the fire. 'Now stop yer crying and listen to me, darling. Yer nothing like your pa, is that clear?'

Marianne wiped her eyes. 'Not at all?'

'Not one little bit. You've got yer ma's lovely ways, my pet. If you'd bin like him, I'd have put you in a home straight away.'

And Nan had been proved right. OK she could be a bit sharp-tongued at times, but this was a minor fault and you had to stand up for yourself in this world. Marianne ran her fingers through her hair. Where'd she get these curls from? Him, she bet. And definitely his brown eyes, because both Renée and Nan had blue eyes.

Marianne yawned and stretched. Time for bed. She was tired and it had been a long and stressful day.

Boris's place was outside in his kennel, but she couldn't face being on her own tonight so she shoved him out for a quick run round and a pee and waited for him with the door ajar. A bitter wind snapped around her ankles and lifted the threadbare carpet, the candle wavered and from somewhere there came a chilling wail of a woman in torment.

Hackles raised, ears flat against his head, Boris shot past her into the broom cupboard. Her heart beating violently, Marianne slammed shut the door and stood leaning against it for support. Franz could say what he liked, but there was such a thing as ghosts and they were out there right now and she wasn't budging from the kitchen until morning.

'Boris,' she called feebly, but the cowardly animal wouldn't budge from the cupboard. Some guard dog. Marianne wondered if he'd be any good if she ever found herself in a dangerous situation. Well he'd proved his stuff saving Gerald, so she just had to hope he'd be as fearless on her behalf. And animals sensed things so he had as much right to be frightened of ghosts as she was.

Marianne made herself a cup of Oxo, banked up the fire with coal slack, settled down in the fireside chair and covered herself with her coat. But it kept slipping off and the arms of the chair jabbed painfully into her ribs. Marianne gave up and tried the floor. This was even worse, hard and draughty. So it was back to the chair. Eventually she fell into a shallow sleep only to be awakened by horses galloping past the house. Marianne started up. The phantom hunt! But no, it was the ill-fitting windows rattling in their frames. Her bones were now so stiff she hardly knew where to put herself. However she did manage to doze off again, but this time golden-eyed wolves stalked the corridors, nearer ... and nearer they came, howling and scrabbling and leaning their heavy bodies against the door. Her own screams woke her, and the scrabbling became fists and feet against wood, the howls a male voice bellowing, 'For Christ's sake, open up,' orchestrated with tugs on the doorbell.

Her fear became contempt. 'No prizes for guessing who that is, Boris,' she said, hauling a sulky dog out of the cupboard and into the snow. 'Our lord and master well and truly plastered by the sound of it.' Marianne ran her fingers through her hair, smoothed her dress and passing from the kitchen into the hall, she was aware of the beginning of a drab dawn.

'It's probably easier to get into the Tower of London than this bloody house,' her employer exploded and pushed past her.

But Marianne was damned if she was going to be intimidated. Following him into the kitchen, she said, 'As you are aware, Captain Lacey, I'm here on my own. There are also some funny customers roaming the countryside and I don't want to be found in my bed with my throat cut, so I made the house secure.'

'You read too many of the wrong books.'

'That's got nothing to do with it; it's called taking sensible precautions and I don't see anything wrong with that.'

Marianne braced herself for another outburst. Instead he dumped a carrier bag on the kitchen table. 'Light the fire in the drawing room and bring me some breakfast.'

'Have you been to see Gerald?'

'Not yet.'

'I thought ...'

He turned. 'I don't pay you to think, Armstrong; I pay you to run this house.'

'He's got pneumonia and that's serious,' Marianne persisted.

'Doctor Gibb has already informed me of the state of my son's health, thank you. As I said, I'd like something to eat. With freezing fog to add to the conditions, it's been hell getting here. On two occasions I nearly ended up in a ditch.'

Shouldn't drink then, should you? she mouthed to his back. 'I'm afraid it'll have to be tea and toast, sir, I haven't got much else in the way of food.'

'Look in the carrier bag; you'll find every thing you need for a breakfast,' he answered, and marched off to the drawing room. Several breakfasts, in fact. Marianne discovered: a horseshoe of black pudding, some sausages and a good pound of bacon. Black market, of course. *Funny how he can always find the money for life's little luxuries, and booze and petrol, but not my wages.*

The fire was already laid and as she struck a match and watched the paper curl, Marianne wondered why her employer couldn't have managed to light it. Too hung-over, she supposed. She glanced across at him. He was stretched out on the sofa, one of the few pieces of furniture he'd failed to sell. Not hard to see why. Horsehair stuffing bulged from split seams and woodworm had gnawed the frame almost to dust. In Marianne's opinion, the best place for it would be the rubbish dump.

Although his eyes were closed Marianne knew he wasn't asleep. Resenting the fact that he was using up her precious stock of logs, she banged around with the fire irons, poking and sweeping and making just enough noise to irritate him. Eventually he sat up, pressed his fingers into his temples and said tightly, 'Go and cook my breakfast.'

Marianne hated being alone in the house, but she dreaded even more her employer's company. At least the household ghosts hadn't harmed her so far, she reflected, as she cracked an egg on the edge of the frying pan and dropped it into the bacon fat. Hugo Lacey, on the other hand, was unpredictable, bordering on dangerous when he was drunk, which was now an almost permanent state.

Marianne sliced the black pudding, adding a couple for herself and gobbling them down before she took the captain's breakfast into him. He was leaning forward staring into the fire with a look of such bleak despair that Marianne's irritation faded into pity. Lost in his own private hell, it was a moment before he became aware of her. 'Oh, it's you,' he said and quickly adjusted his features.

The upkeep of this crumbling pile, the debts, Gerald's illness; he was breaking up under the burden of it all; and using whisky as a cure-all, not a good idea. Marianne placed the tray on a low table beside him. 'Here you are, sir, just what the doctor ordered, three rashers of bacon, sausages, some black pudding and a good strong pot of tea.'

He managed a 'thank you', then took up his knife and fork. Leaving him to it, Marianne got on with the daily chores of feeding the chickens and bringing in wood. She was eating her own meagre breakfast when he put his head round the door.

'I'm off to the hospital to see Gerald now.'

Marianne jumped up and hastily swallowed a mouthful of toast. 'Oh. Please give him my love, sir, and tell him I'll visit him as soon as I can … and drive carefully.'

That was a pointless piece of advice, Marianne thought as she heard the wheels skid off down the drive. He drove with such a suicidal recklessness; Marianne wondered whether he ever stopped to reflect on what would become of his only child if he had a fatal accident. No, too self-centred, too wrapped up in his own misery to consider Gerald's future welfare and who might look after him.

And *who* would? She chewed on a piece of toast and thought.

She'd hate to see the poor little devil in an orphanage and there must be a few relatives around, even if none had turned up for Mrs Lacey's funeral. It also followed that there'd be some names and addresses around, very likely in Hugo's office; not that she would dare go raking about in there and anyway it was locked and strictly out of bounds when he wasn't at home. Of course, there were the photograph albums; they might throw up some of information, and also the diaries, she wasn't sure how many at the moment, but they could prove fruitful.

Deterred by the polar conditions and power cuts, Marianne hadn't been near the attic recently and it was so cold today that she just grabbed a an assortment of albums and diaries, hurried back down to the kitchen and spread them out on the table. Here she could do a thorough investigation in her own good time and maybe dig up some interesting information.

It was impossible to establish whether any of the people in the photographs were Laceys, neither was any indication given of where they might live. In fact, it seemed a disappointing haul, and there were none of those huge family gatherings that the Laceys had appeared to enjoy so much in the past. In fact the family had rather petered out, and there wasn't a single clue that might lead her to any relatives.

Marianne was about ready to give up when she opened the last album. This was more like it: Hugo in various stages of childhood riding to hounds, then at some posh public school looking a proper toff in a top hat and striped trousers. He even sported a walking-stick. That must have been before the money ran out, because you couldn't send a child to a public school on coat buttons.

Marianne turned the page. Hugo had now moved on to university and the photographs showed a young man enjoying life to the full, playing cricket, punting on the river, fooling around on the lawn of some grand house with a group of young men and women, all in fancy dress. But what was really remarkable was Hugo's obvious happiness. It burst from the photographs, a man in love. Astoundingly handsome, too, a deb's delight.

After that the pages were blank, no wedding photographs, not even a record of Gerald's birth or christening. It was obvious, though, that the pages had once held photographs, but that they had been ripped out, and in some anger, because many of the pages were torn. It didn't take the head of Scotland Yard to work out why either: Felicity.

Marianne turned back to the earlier photos. She must be in that circle of friends. She studied the group in fancy dress closely. Hugo wore a matador's outfit, so it made sense that the girl dressed as a Spanish dancer was his partner. And she was pretty. But so were all the girls, glowing with the health and confidence that came with money. Felicity could be any one of them and surely she had relatives who would look after her son? Marianne had just turned her investigator's eye on the girls in the punt when she heard a car. Lifting her head, she listened. He was back. Oh, God almighty. She gathered up the albums and diaries, slung them in the larder, and was closing the door as Hugo Lacey and Franz walked through the door.

Astonished, Marianne glanced from one to the other.

'Met him at the back door. Claims he's come to find out how Gerald is, but I wasn't born yesterday,' Hugo Lacey sneered.

Marianne blushed at the insinuation and Franz, looking deeply uncomfortable, stared at the far wall.

'Never trust a Nazi, my dear; rape and pillage are all they're good for.'

Franz rounded on him with clenched fists. 'Do not call me a Nazi,' he warned.

Hugo Lacey's face came up close to Franz's. 'Nazi!' he spat and Franz's fist shot out and hit him on the chin.

Drink had made her employer unsteady on his feet and

Marianne watched appalled as he staggered back in bleary surprise. 'Oh Franz, you shouldn't have,' she wailed. 'He'll report you now.'

Aware of the enormity of what he'd done, the colour had leeched from Franz's skin, but the muscles in his jaw were tight with rage. 'I do not care. He should not have insulted me.'

It had been a glancing blow and Hugo recovered his balance and came right back with fingers bunched. In an effort to prevent it developing into a fist fight, with blood on the ground, Marianne ran and stood between them. 'Stop it! You're behaving like schoolboys instead of grown men,' she screamed at them both.

'Do you really think I'd touch him? But you'll care all right by the time I've finished with you, Nazi. You've just attacked a serving officer and your camp commandant will hear of this, and it will give me the greatest pleasure to have you put on a charge.'

'And I will tell him what a British army officer called me,' Franz retorted, and walked out of the door.

Sensing that it might not help his cause, Marianne had to force herself not to run after him. Never mind that he'd been provoked, he'd struck an army officer, and there would be repercussions.

Enraged on Franz's behalf, she rounded on Hugo Lacey. 'Why did you say that to him? You had no right.'

He stared at her suspiciously. 'There is something going on between you two, isn't there? Or you wouldn't jump to his defence like that.'

Marianne stared straight back. 'There is not,' she lied, 'but that's our supply of logs just gone. Franz came regularly – and in his free time, to chop wood for us, so pray for a thaw or we're likely to freeze to death. Unless,' she added, 'you're prepared to do it.'

'Not my thing. Don't worry your little head about it, I'll get hold of some coal,' he said airily, 'but I'm going to rest now.'

Marianne followed him. 'When?' she persisted.

He fell on to the sofa. 'Later, after I've seen Gerald.'

'But I thought that's where you'd been, to the hospital.'

'Didn't get round to it,' he mumbled.

'What do you mean, didn't get round to it?'

'Got delayed.'

'At the Plough and Harrow I suppose.'

He opened one eye and held up his index finger. 'Right, first time,' he smirked, turned on his side and slept.

Chapter Thirteen

When Marianne looked at the calendar and saw that eight days had passed without a visit from Franz, she knew that her employer had done what he'd threatened and reported him. Incensed by the injustice of it, Marianne brooded about it for ten minutes, decided he shouldn't be allowed to get away with it, and went and looked for a pen, paper and ink in the library. As an afterthought she picked up a dictionary. She had witnessed the incident and if she didn't speak up for Franz after what he'd done for her, she knew that, for the rest of her life, she'd remember and feel ashamed.

But it was a bit daunting, writing to someone in authority, and she didn't want to be dismissed as an ignoramus, so Marianne made good use of the dictionary. She also thought carefully before committing her opinion of the incident to paper. However, once she'd decided how she would word it she dipped the pen in the ink then, in her best handwriting, she began, and the words flowed.

Dear Commandant
Excuse me for my cheek in writing to you but I want you to
know that Franz Hartmann socked my employer Captain
Hugo Lacey because he called him Nazi and other words so
horrible my pen won't let me write them down and I know all

this because I was there. Maybe Franz shouldn't have lost his temper but it was only a jab and he had a good reason to be offended because you see, Hitler's thugs put Franz's father in prison and he died soon after he came out. I hope this helps you see Franz's point of view and to understand how insulted he felt. I also hope you won't lock him up for too long because he is a good man and a hard worker and doesn't deserve it.

She signed her name, *Marianne Armstrong (Miss)*, read the letter through, added a comma or two, then shoved it in to an envelope and walked to the village to post it before she lost her nerve. It was a rare day of sunshine, a rapidly thawing, glistening watery world of gushing streams and flooded meadows, a day to put a spring in the step and lighten the heart. Under a hummock of melting snow Marianne noticed a clump of snowdrops pushing their way through and the sight of these fragile flowers challenging winter filled her with a rare sense of optimism. Real little fighters and if they could do it so could she. Maybe, too, they're telling me the worst of the weather's behind us and spring is around the corner. And perhaps Renée will write soon telling me she's on her way home.

Well, the camp commandant is about to hear from me, thought Marianne. She went to slip the letter into the post box and was overtaken by doubt. I could be making it far worse for Franz, interfering like this. But he hasn't got anyone else to stick up for him and no one who cares about him as much as I do. I've told the truth and if there is any justice, he'll be let off his punishment. The envelope slid from her fingers and she heard it land with a plop. The deed was done. She turned away and crossed the road to the butcher's.

Unusually there wasn't a queue. In fact Marianne was Mr Veal's only customer. 'And how's our young gentleman coming along?' the butcher enquired, bringing his cleaver down on a leg of pork.

'His father doesn't tell me a lot, but I saw Doctor Gibb in the village the other day and he said he's doing nicely. If the weather stays like this I'm going to visit him tomorrow.'

'Pop in on your way, I'd like to send him along a little something.'

'That's kind of you, Mr Veal.'

'Well … poor little beggar.'

'Mr Veal …'

'Yes, me dook?'

Marianne hesitated and then blurted out, 'I sometimes get the feeling that Captain Lacey doesn't love Gerald like he should.'

'Do you now?'

'Is there any reason?'

'Well, yes there is, but I don't know if I can say and it's a bit of a long story.'

Long or not, Marianne wanted to hear it, every single detail, so egging him on, she asked, 'Did you know Gerald's mother?'

'I did.'

'What was she like?'

Mr Veal paused. 'What was she like? Now there's a question. Beautiful, reckless, extravagant – Lord, could she spend, and adored by everyone, men and women alike.'

'Is she dead?'

'For all I know she might be. Maybe he murdered her and buried her in the cellar.'

Marianne licked her lips nervously. 'Do you mean Captain Lacey?'

'I in't one to gossip, but nobody would have blamed him, not after what she done. I never saw a man love a woman like 'e did her. Worshipped the ground she walked on, and she betrayed that love.'

'In what way?'

'Got herself up the spout with some air force chappie.'

'You mean she had a baby with another man?'

Mr Veal laughed. 'Surprised you, did I?'

'A bit,' Marianne admitted, but not as much as Mr Veal imagined, because she had the letter and knew of the man's (her lover) desperate passion for Felicity.

'I wasn't really serious about Captain Lacey doin' her in. More likely she ran off with her Brylcreem boy. It was after that that Mr Lacey took against Gerald. I think he got it in his head that if she'd done it with one man, there could be others and Gerald might not be his.'

'But Gerald's the spitting image of his grandma.'

'Tell that to a man whose pride has been stamped on and who's dying inside with grief.'

The bell over the door jangled, a customer walked in and Mr Veal became more businesslike in tone. 'Now what can I do for you, Maid Marion? A nice pork chop suit you?'

Outside, Marianne paused on the step. In spite of knowing a fragment of the story, Mr Veal's further revelations still shocked her. That woman, the damage she's done, she thought censoriously, and driven her husband to drink. She couldn't even be bothered to keep in touch with her son. A lost soul of a boy who's forbidden to speak his mother's name, who longs for her desperately and now lies critically ill in hospital. But being the flighty type it would be off with the old and on with the new and that air force bod and their child would have all Felicity's love now. Poor Gerald, with two parents, but neither of whom cared a toss for him.

She wrote to him regularly, tried to cheer him up with funny drawings and stories of Boris, sent him Franz's love, but that didn't make up for all the instability Gerald had endured in his short life. No wonder he often played up. Snow or not, tomorrow she'd go and visit him, Marianne decided, and she set off across the green to check the bus timetable and what number bus she needed to get to the hospital.

She was almost home when she heard the coalman and his horse Harold come clop-clop up the drive. It was such a rare visit that Boris got all excited and started chasing his tail, and Marianne was so pleased to see them she wanted to kiss Mr Berridge's coal-blackened face.

'How much can we have, Mr Berridge?' Marianne asked, hoping her smile would earn an extra sack of coal.

'Half a hundredweight.'

'Is that all?'

'Thank yer lucky stars you've got this,' the coalman retorted. He heaved a sack on to his back and tipped it into the coal hole. 'The weather's returning to its old ways tomorrow, so yer not likely see me for a while. I don't know how the government expects me to run a business with no bloomin' coal,' he grumbled. He climbed on to his cart, ordered Harold to 'walk on', and trundled back down the drive.

In spite of Mr Berridge's weather predictions, Marianne was determined nothing would stop her visiting Gerald. So, obstinately ignoring the steadily falling snow, the following morning she packed a *Beano*, a *Dandy* and a bag of mint humbugs into a carrier bag and set off for the village.

She'd been waiting at the bus stop for over half an hour, when a man in one of the cottages came to his gate and called, 'I should go home, pet. I've heard on the wireless that it's so bad south of here nothing's getting through from Leicester and you'll catch yer death if you stand there much longer.'

It was sound advice and Marianne thanked him for it, but she could imagine Gerald at this very minute, sitting up in bed, pale but hopeful as the visitors' bell rang. Then family and friends would push through the door and race each other down the ward, waving, calling out, kissing, hugging, exclaiming at how well their loved one looked, even if the patient was at death's door. So unless she went nobody would stop at Gerald's bed, and eventually that spark of hope would vanish and he would turn on his side, cover his head and sob into his pillow. She owed it to him to get to the hospital and a bus might come. Stamping her feet and jumping up and down to keep the blood flowing, Marianne gave it a another half-hour then, conceding that the man was right and she would catch her death if she stood there any longer, she trailed back to Hope Grange, feeling wretched for letting Gerald down. Her employer's car outside the house didn't help her mood either.

'What's he doing home?' she asked Boris, who'd come to meet her. Then she remembered the damning letter and regretted her impulsive action. She really couldn't face him and his temper. Without having much idea where she would go, Marianne was about to walk away, when the door opened. 'Ah, there you are, Armstrong. I wondered where you'd got to.' Hugo Lacey held the door open wide, and she had no choice but to walk through it.

His tone was genial, which meant he didn't know about the letter. Marianne breathed easily again. 'I've been trying to get to the hospital to see Gerald, but there weren't any buses, so I had to give up.'

'Well, never mind, I've been to see him.'

'How is he?'

'Quite chirpy, and ready to come home. The nurse mentioned sometime next week.'

'If you don't mind me saying so, sir, he'd be better staying where he is. If he comes back here he could fall ill again, because a few logs and a half a hundredweight of coal is all I've got to keep this house warm and there's no telling when we'll get another delivery.'

Hugo Lacey gave a shrug. 'We'll have to manage as best we can, won't we? And now I've got work to do in my office.'

'Captain Lacey …'

He turned slowly. 'Yes?'

'I don't suppose you could drive me to the hospital to see Gerald.'

Taken aback by her forthright request, he had to struggle to think up an excuse. 'Sorry, I'm low on petrol. I've just enough to get me back to camp.'

Funny how, in spite of petrol coupons, this had never been a problem in the past.

'In the meantime, bring me a pot of tea, Armstrong.'

Since there wasn't much to detain him, Marianne expected her employer to deal with any business matters and then leave, to visit the carmine-mouthed, red-taloned floozy of her imagination, now that she knew he wasn't engaged in anything top secret. However, he was still there at four in the afternoon, sitting at his desk with the oil heater against his legs, going through the brown envelopes that had lain unopened for weeks, then writing, writing, writing.

'Are you staying, sir?' Marianne asked, after he'd rung for yet another pot of tea.

He stood up, rubbed his neck and flexed his fingers, then went to the window and pulled back a tattered red velvet curtain. 'Yes. I daren't risk going out in this weather, I could easily find myself stranded.'

'It'll have to be Spam fritters for tea.'

He let the curtain fall and turned. 'Spam fritters?' He sounded surprised that such delicacies existed. 'I suppose that will do. Armstrong, before you go … There's something I need to tell you, something that will affect your future. I'm selling Hope Grange.'

Marianne took a shocked step backwards. Talk about a bombshell. She knew it was all going to the dogs, but even so ... 'S ... selling?' she stuttered. 'But where will you go? What about me?' She planned to leave, but wanted it to be in her own good time.

'There's no immediate hurry but I would advise you to start looking for another situation. With your culinary skills I'm sure you'll have no trouble finding one, and I promise I will give you a glowing reference. As for Gerald and me, well we'll have to wait until the sale goes through, see if there's any money left. To think,' he went on, his voice hard with contempt, 'that soon this house will be rubble and council houses will stand in its place and ignorant people who keep their coal in the bath will live here. A swing of a ball and chain and two hundred years of tradition, two hundred years of the Lacey family ... gone.' He choked on the last word, then glared accusingly at Marianne. 'It's your bloody socialist government's fault, do you know that? Their vicious taxes are making paupers of the people who've always been the backbone of this country.' The veins in his neck bulged, a sure sign that he was working himself up into a fine old rage.

'Don't blame me,' Marianne answered robustly. 'It's not my government. I'm too young to vote.' She bet it never occurred to him that the government caused her plenty of problems, too, with the perpetual struggle she had to get hold of fuel and put food on the table. Of course it didn't, he was too wrapped up in self-pity to notice anyone else's problems.

'I'll say this for Mr Attlee; he's promised to look after us from the cradle to the grave, so at least people's teeth won't rot and fall out because they can't afford a dentist.'

'Yes, and who's paying for it?' He dug his index finger into his chest. 'Me.' On a real rant now, he went on, 'They want equality, the great unwashed, but they'll see how well they get on without our kind. I predict that in ten years this country will be run by communists and on its knees.'

It seemed to Marianne that the country was already on its

knees and as for the communists, well she had more important things on her mind, such as that shortly she would find herself homeless and jobless. And as for that jibe about the poor keeping their coal in the bath, well chance would be a fine thing. An outside lav and the scullery sink to wash in had been their lot, although Nan, being a stickler for cleanliness, would march her down to the public baths every Saturday afternoon.

And by the sound of it her employer was about to get a taste of how the poor lived. Perhaps he would realize then that people were often brought low by circumstances beyond their control. Marianne shot him a glance. The handsome features were hard and the bitter line of the mouth said it all. How could a world that had held such promise have let him down so badly?

'I'll go and get tea ready,' she said, and sensing his mood wasn't going to improve, she slid out of the door before he started using her for target practice.

When she got back to the kitchen she saw that, in her hurry, she'd left an album she'd been thumbing through out on the table. She shoved it in the table drawer. Phew, good job he didn't come in here, Although he'd probably forgotten all about the albums and where they were stored, he'd still kick up a fuss if he discovered she'd been poking around in his family's private affairs.

She never knew what mood he would be in, although it was rarely a good one and this in turn made her edgy, as she was at this moment. Sitting down, Marianne massaged her shoulders and neck, then closed her eyes and breathed deeply and slowly. *Actually I'm glad I'm leaving this place before that man turns me into a nervous wreck.* And live-in jobs were two a penny so first thing tomorrow she would go down to the village, buy a copy of *The Lady*, and see what the magazine had to offer in the way of work in this part of the world or London.

Feeling better for having made a decision, Marianne stood up and started whisking batter for the fritters. She dipped the slices of Spam into the mixture then, one by one, into the heated fat and watched them brown and crisp. This ought to improve his mood, she thought, and placed the fritters on a plate. Marianne hesitated over the peas, because in spite of an overnight soak and a long simmer, they were still on the hard side. In the end she added them, mainly to fill the plate.

Laying out a tray she took it through to her employer.

'What's this?' he asked, scowling at the food.

'Spam fritters and peas, like I said.'

He gave a sort of grunt, picked up his knife and fork, cut a wedge of fritter and chased the peas around the plate. Unfortunately every time he tried to spear one, it shot off across the room.

'Bloody muck!' Hugo Lacey took a swipe at the plate with the flat of his hand and sent it spinning across the room. The congealing fritters hit the far wall, then, in a leisurely fashion, slithered down it, while the peas sprayed the room like bullets from a machine gun.

Marianne watched dumbstruck. She only had a limited patience and this was the end of the road. 'You made the mess, you can clean it up,' she snapped and marched out of the room. He could stew. Tonight she would pack, and first thing in the morning leave this place, get the bus to Leicester, then a train to London. There was that girls' hostel in the New Kent Road, it was expensive but the money she'd saved would see her through until she got herself sorted out. As Marianne made her plans, life at once seemed simpler. At least it did if she ignored a sick boy, the man she loved, an aunt halfway across the world and one dog.

Chapter Fourteen

Boris stared balefully at Marianne, but she refused to meet his eye. Her suitcase was packed, she was leaving first thing tomorrow and no dog could stop her.

Soon after his childish tantrums with the food, Hugo had turned to his old comforter the whisky bottle and before long was as soused as a herring. He raged, he roared, all his misfortunes were the fault of the government, the lower orders and that whore – Felicity, Marianne assumed. Then came the familiar sound of breaking bottles, accompanied by language a true gentleman would never use.

He was now a danger to himself and to her, and Marianne didn't want to be here when the dam burst. Her stomach muscles were like knotted rope, but by and large her contempt kept fear at bay. However, poor old Boris was reduced to a cowed and shivering wreck. He came and huddled against Marianne and she rubbed his ears and spoke to him softly and wondered what his history was. A cruel owner somewhere in his past, she supposed. 'It's all right, old chap, the only harm he's doing is to himself.' But this was no consolation to Boris and he was still trembling long after the uproar had subsided.

She was weary to the bone; her lids began to droop and she longed to fall into bed, cover her head and forget all this in sleep. But Marianne knew that the sight of her might set Hugo Lacey off into another rage, so she waited and after a while things did quieten down. Tiptoeing across the hall she found the courage to pause at the office door. Silence. She opened it a fraction. The floor was strewn with ripped-up brown envelopes, and Hugo lay with his head slumped forward on the desk. Well, it was one way of dealing with the problem of debt, she supposed, and closed the door on him for the last time.

That had been last night and now she was packed and ready to go, thankful to be leaving this house, with its ghosts, secrets and unhappiness. Her future might be uncertain, but at least she'd be in control of it.

Her soon to be ex-employer was up because she could hear him moving about, probably with a thundering headache and a mouth like a sewer. Well, it served him right, and she'd never feel sorry for him again, not after what he had done to Franz, whom, thanks to him, she would probably never see again.

But it was unlikely that his hangover would do anything to improve his mood and she had to go in and ask for her wages. To ease her path, Marianne made him a pot of tea, then, bracing herself, she knocked and walked in. The room smelt of booze, and bits of the brown envelopes stuck to the soles of her shoes. His skin was grey like putty, his features ill-tempered, his clothes crumpled and he was badly in need of a shave and probably a bath.

'Good morning sir,' she said briskly.

He scowled at her. 'What's good about it?'

'Well, I've brought you a pot of tea.'

'Put it there.'

Marianne placed the tray where he'd indicated.

He tapped the cup with his forefinger. 'Pour it.'

Rude blighter. But she did as he ordered then stood back and waited for him to drink it. When he'd finished, Marianne cleared her throat. 'Captain Lacey, I've come to tell you that I'm leaving your service today.'

His head came up, but too quickly and he winced. 'Leaving? Today?'

'Yes, this morning on the eleven o'clock bus.'

'But that's preposterous; I'm not ready for you to go. Gerald's due home any time now and someone will have to look after him.'

'Afraid it won't be me. Your news about the house and everything came as a shock, but now I've had time to think it over I realize it's better for me to go sooner than later. I've no family to speak of, so I need to find a place to live and a job as quickly as possible otherwise I could end up homeless, and I shall start by returning to London.'

'And I'm in the army and have important duties to attend to.'

Marianne gave an exasperated sigh. She might as well have been talking to a brick wall for all the understanding he showed of her situation. 'I'm sure the army will give you compassionate leave if you explain about Gerald. Or you could employ someone from the village.'

'No one will come up here from the village,' he muttered.

Now I wonder why? Didn't pay them, perhaps? 'I'm sorry, I don't know what else to suggest. But if you could make up my wages, plus holiday money, I'll be in to collect it in half an hour.'

His look was horrible to behold. 'Holiday money? You'll get no holiday money, now get out!' He pointed to the door.

It took courage, but Marianne stood firm. His bully-boy tactics cut no ice with her. No more shilly-shallying, the time had come to speak out. 'It's what was agreed, and I have your letter to prove it. Two and six for every month of service and I've worked hard for this family, put up with a lot, especially last night.' There, she'd said it.

'Last night?'

'Yes, you throwing good food at the wall. And then there was your drunken behaviour. I've never heard language like it before, not even in Camberwell.'

He glowered at her. 'Drunken behaviour? Me? I don't know what you're talking about, woman.'

'So I suppose it was a poltergeist that smashed the bottles, tore up these bills and envelopes?'

He didn't answer. 'You shall have your holiday money, Armstrong. Now please leave me.'

With pleasure. Outside his office Marianne leaned against the wall and closed her eyes. God, she deserved a medal for telling it to him straight like that.

It was hard to think of food after all the high drama, but knowing she had a long journey ahead of her, Marianne managed to get a plate of porridge down before starting on her final task of letter-writing.

The first was to Gerald. Without going into any details, Marianne told him she was returning to London, but hoped to come back and see him before long, and in the meantime he was to look after Boris. The second letter was to Franz. She found this the most difficult to write and she chewed on her pen for a long time. At last she poured out her heart to him, telling him about Hope Grange being sold and demolished, about Hugo Lacey's out-of-control drinking, which had left her with no choice but to leave. Lastly, she told him she loved him very much and even though she was returning to London, she hoped they'd have a chance to see each other before he was sent back Germany. As she signed the letter and added twenty kisses, a tear rolled down her cheek and on to the paper. It was a hopeless situation; there was little chance of them ever meeting again and there was no point in pretending they would.

Marianne printed SWALK across the back of the sealed envelope, then cried some more. And once she'd started she couldn't stop and she cried because the crazy thing was that, although she'd grown to hate the house, this was where she'd found love.

None of this nonsense, she told herself severely. In a couple of hours you are going to walk out of that door and not look back. Marianne blew her nose, wiped her eyes and settled down to scribble her last letter, a note to Renée with the address of the hostel near the Elephant and Castle, where she hoped to get a room.

After so many unfulfilled promises, Marianne knew there wasn't much chance of her aunt turning up here, but if she did and found a pile of rubble instead of a house and no niece, with memories of the war still vivid, it might not do Renée's heart a lot of good.

Franz and Gerald's letters she would pop in the pillar box before she caught the bus, then she would ask Mr Veal to hold on to Renée's. If, by the slightest chance her aunt did turn up here and started making enquiries, it was the butcher to whom people would direct her.

At last she was done. Marianne laid the envelopes out on the table, then sat back and drummed her fingers. Time was passing and still no money. It was deliberate of course. He knew she had a bus and train to catch and was making sure she missed them. She'd give him ten minutes, then go and hammer on the door. If this was what Felicity had to put up with: drinking, unreasonable behaviour, no wonder she'd run off with another man. Marianne sat up. *Oh my Lord, the photograph albums.* Somehow she had to sneak them back up to the attic, for if Hugo discovered that a servant had been rifling through his personal belongings teasing out family secrets, the feathers would fly.

The attic was clogged with stuff, most of it junk which, if it couldn't be sold, would probably end up on the rubbish dump. And along with it would go the albums, and Gerald's family history and a precious record of past times. For a moment

Marianne toyed with the idea of holding on to them, but common sense told her it was impossible, for not even one album would fit into her small suitcase. There were the stables, of course. Yes and she'd have to traipse back downstairs and risk getting caught; furthermore she had a bus to catch. Marianne knelt, lifted the trunk lid and replaced the albums with a real sense of loss. But the diary and drawings, she decided, had to be saved for Gerald, and those who came after him, especially now that the house was about to be demolished. Besides, Barbara was an interesting young woman and she wanted to know more about her and that flighty cousin of hers who'd chosen a rough and ready navvy, a young man whom Barbara clearly didn't approve of. Perching herself on the lid of the trunk, Marianne opened the diary at random.

STRETTON MAGNA FEAST DAY JUNE 1846 was written in bold lettering across two pages followed by: *Hugo Lacey attended church this morning with his father, the squire. I wonder why? Could it be Anna? And why is she wearing red shoes? What is she trying to say?*

Her curiosity quickened, Marianne turned the page, but Barbara had clearly lost interest in her cousin and instead she had filled the pages with dazzling colour. The bit of soggy grass that had been the village green exploded into life. The fairground people were erecting their merry-go-rounds, swing-boats and penny peepshows, and dotted amongst them were stalls selling gingerbread, trinkets and lemonade, while a cheapjack set out his pots and pans on the grass, and a sign read; Madame Ocardie, World Famous Clairvoyant, Palms Read For One Penny.

The next page was a wonder of golden sunshine, bees, butterflies and morris men. Marianne sighed. If only she could step out of her own cold, dreary world into that peaceful, sun-filled magical, perfect day.

Further on Barbara had sketched two men in a roped-off area, wrestling. *The Great Bear and Jack Ellis, stripped to their waists,* she'd written.

The comments that followed were:

Anna took a great interest in Jack as he stepped into the ring, pulled off his shirt, rolled it up, then threw it into the crowd. Several young girls, maidservants probably, made to grab it and there was a rather unseemly tussle, which I was relieved to see Anna had enough sense not to engage in. Our family are landowners in a small way and she should try and remember that. But then Anna has always been perverse, who but she would purchase red shoes? It hasn't stopped her ogling Jack's bare torso, though. I do not care for the man but he is strong and he has grappled the Great Bear to the ground three times and won the prize money of half a sovereign. Now his following of serving girls has doubled and they all have stars in their eyes.

A ragamuffin, no doubt a navvy child, has been caught red-handed stealing gingerbread from a stall and is being chastised by Squire Lacey and threatened with a flogging or the stocks. But I see that the squire has relented and allowed the little thief to go free. I also notice that to mollify the stall-holder, he has handed her some coins and there is now much bowing and scraping. Hugo is following Anna around without much success, which is foolish of her because, although he is known to be a degenerate, sooner or later he will become squire of Hope Grange.

All morris men drunk, apart from Jethro the fiddler who, being Methody, does not allow ale to touch his lips. But he has struck up a jig on his fiddle and is moving off across the green with young and old, male and female, skipping along behind him. When he finds a smooth area of grass Jethro stops and calls for everyone's attention. 'Right longways for

*as many as will and we'll have "Haste to the Wedding".'
Immediately two lines are formed and I watch and envy, but
many of the men of the village are of stunted growth and I am
tall so I do not expect to find a partner. Instead I observe and
sketch and I take note that Anna has disappeared. I hear a
voice and look up. 'Good afternoon Miss Lawrence.' It is the
squire holding out his hand and smiling. 'Would you care to
join in the dance?' I rise to my feet and see, with a sense of
gratitude, that he stands two inches or more above me. The
squire shows no sign of tiredness in spite of his age, which I
take to be forty-five years or thereabouts. There is whispering
behind hands, but I do not care, for Felix has invited me up
to Hope Grange to see his collection of orchids.*

*This morning my happiness is clouded briefly by the news
that there was a robbery last night out on the Queen's
Highway and a gentleman was relieved of his purse...*

Chapter Fifteen

'Am I disturbing you?'
Startled by the intrusion, Marianne let the sketchbook slip from her fingers. It landed at her employer's feet and he stooped to pick it up. 'Prying into my family's affairs, I see.' He flicked over the pages.

'No, no I'm not.'

'So what else could have brought you up here?'

'I … I was looking for a box. My suitcase, it's a bit on the small side and I've run out of space.'

'A box, eh? And while you were about it you thought you'd have a nose around. But tell me, were you gripped by the sordid details?'

'I told you I haven't read it.'

'Well, don't let me stop you. Here, finish it.' He pushed the sketchbook at her. 'It'll show you exactly what the fair sex is capable of.'

Marriane took a step backwards. 'Thank you, but I won't have time.'

'And why is this?'

'You know why: because I'm leaving as soon as you've paid me.'

'Ah, yes, your wages. I'm afraid you'll have to wait for those. Unfortunately I'm a bit short at present.'

She felt her hackles rise. 'But you promised.' This was unfair. 'I don't believe you. That money's mine by right and I won't be able to manage without it. There's my train fare, lodgings, food, unless you expect me to sleep on the streets.'

'Frankly it would cause me a great deal of inconvenience if you were to go, so rest assured you will have a roof over your head tonight.'

'I want my money, right now, and then I want to leave,' she repeated.

'Quite impossible.'

'You can't force me to stay.'

'Oh yes I can.' He dangled two keys in front of her. 'I've locked the front and back doors.'

'How dare you! Give them to me.' Marianne tried to snatch the keys from him, but he lifted them out of her reach.

'Naughty, naughty.' He wagged a finger at her.

'You're holding me against my will and I'll report you to the police, and you'll go to prison for this, just you see,' Marianne threatened. She charged, pushing against his chest with all her force. Normally it would have been as pointless as a flea attacking a hippo, but Hugo was still hung over and unsteady on his feet and, taken unawares, he staggered back, giving Marianne the chance to shoot past him down the stairs. She could hear him behind her, cursing, but with no time to figure out the safest place to be, she headed for the kitchen, slammed the door and leaned against it, her heart going nineteen to the dozen.

Pleased to see her, Boris came ambling over and pressed a damp nose into her hand. 'Get in the broom cupboard,' Marianne hissed, feeling the pressure of Hugo's shoulder against the door. It flew open and as she stumbled across the kitchen Marianne was relieved to see the tip of Boris's tail disappearing from view.

The table broke her fall, but she was winded. Righting herself, she saw that the letters she'd written to Gerald, Franz and Renée had been ripped open and scattered all over the table. *The pig.*

Hugo sauntered in, a bottle tucked under one arm, the frightful doll under the other. 'Annie, our little friend, found her in the cellar.' He propped her up in a chair. Marianne shuddered and backed away, but he grabbed her wrists and forced her into a chair beside the doll. 'She enjoys company, but doesn't get much of it down in that cellar. And if you don't behave you'll be getting a taste of what it's like down there.'

Marianne shivered. 'You wouldn't dare.'

He moved close and stared into her eyes. 'Never ever dare me. Several people have made that mistake and regretted it.' He turned away, bent, and rearranged the doll's moth-eaten dress, then tightened the string that held her red shoes in place. He stood back. 'That's smartened her up a bit. She murdered out of greed and envy, but betrayed herself with those shoes. But you seem interested in my family's affairs, so I'll tell you the whole sordid story.'

'I don't want to hear.' Marianne clapped her hands over her ears.

'I'm warning you ... the cellar, and you could be down there for a long time. If people ask, I'll just say you've returned to London. No one would miss you except your German, and he'll be gone from these shores before long.'

Marianne thought of the dank, dark cellar and silently prayed: *Help me someone, please.* Although who was there? Not Franz, confined to barracks; not Gerald, still in hospital.

Her clearly mad employer sat down and stretched his legs towards the dying fire. 'The local poacher saw it all; Jack Ellis's attack on my namesake, which left him dead, their flight, the whore's loss of one red shoe which, in spite of him being a bit simple, Titus had the good sense to bring up to the house as evidence of this foul deed. It is also recorded that he swore on the

Bible that every word of his story was true. Meanwhile Anna's cousin, Barbara, whose marriage to the squire had taken place that day and who was about to set off on her honeymoon in Paris, discovered that the priceless Lacey jewels, given into her care as was the custom, had gone missing. Immediately a posse set off in pursuit of the thieves.'

Marianne was stunned. Such evil happenings. But she shouldn't be surprised for, after all, the atmosphere of the house had disturbed her that very first time she walked through the door. And then there were the voices and whispers and unaccountable noises.

Hugo Lacey took a swig of whisky and continued: 'But the real tragedy was that those priceless pieces of jewellery were never recovered, neither was our good fortune.' He thumped the table with his fist, and his face grew flushed. 'Just think what I could have done with them: saved this house from destruction, lived the life a gentleman should expect, with servants, a stable of thoroughbreds and my son at Eton.'

He pushed back his chair and began striding around the kitchen. Her nerves taut, Marianne watched the level of whisky fall and his anger rise to a dangerous level. She rubbed her sweating palms down her skirt, knowing that when the blast came, she would be in the firing line.

But there was a good chance that he'd soon be off in search of a refill and then she'd make a run for it. In the meantime she would try and keep him talking.

'What happened to them?'

'Jack Ellis, a common criminal, met the end he deserved and was caught and hanged. He was no loss and I imagine the world became a better place once he left it.'

'What about her?'

'Even though she'd been party to the murder of my namesake and the theft of her cousin's jewels, she escaped the hangman's noose. However, she didn't live to enjoy her ill-gotten gains and died giving birth in a squalid rooming house in Camberwell nine months later. It was said that the brat survived. Anna's father went down to Camberwell and searched for it, but he never found the child. If it did live it would have been sent to an orphanage.'

The fire was low and Marianne shivered from cold and apprehension. She stared at the doll. No wonder the villagers burnt her likeness on Bonfire night. *I've got to get away from this crazy house or I'll soon be as barmy as the rest of them.* 'Could you unlock the back door, please? I need to get more logs for the fire.'

'Think you're going to catch me out with a trick like that, do you?' Hugo pulled a key from his pocket. 'I'll get them.'

Holding herself ready to make a run for it, Marianne eyed the almost empty whisky bottle and watched him weave an irregular path to the door. His hands had a drinker's tremor and he had to make several stabs with the key before he succeeded in inserting it in the lock.

Unfortunately Hugo was still sober enough to anticipate her plans and he squeezed round the door, locking it from the outside. But Marianne wasn't ready to give up. She moved to the window and watched him juggle with an armful of logs and the key, then drop the lot in the snow. Several minutes in freezing temperatures with inanimate objects getting the better of him reduced her employer to a red-eyed fury, and when at last he found the key and unlocked the door, he strode into the kitchen with such a look of menace on his face that Marianne backed away.

He dumped the logs in the hearth, brushed the dirt off his hands and jacket, turned and announced, 'I'm hungry. Get me something to eat.'

'The Spam you threw at the wall was the last of the tinned food.'

'I don't believe you.'

'There's the larder, take a look.'

'You're supposed to run this house.'

'I *used* to run the house,' Marianne corrected, 'and on a very limited income.' As she spoke the lights went out.

'What the devil...?

'A power cut. We get them most days.'

'Christ, this country is going to the dogs. You'd never guess we'd won the war.'

Marianne lit a candle and placed it on the table. 'That's the last one, after that we'll be sitting in the dark.' And so they sat, watching each other, Marianne plotting her escape, he drumming his fingers on the table. Then, abruptly, he pushed back the chair and left the room, locking her in. When he returned, he had a green, gauzy evening dress draped over his arm.

Ill-lit as the room was, Marianne was also aware of a difference in him. His movements were more languid, his features softer, the lips no longer tight with resentment. The aggressive Hugo, Marianne could deal with, this one she found deeply unsettling. He moved his chair close to her and studied her intently. 'It's extraordinary what candlelight does to a woman's face; it gives beauty, mystery even to the most commonplace features.' Reaching out he stroked her cheek.

Disgust ripped through her body and Marianne shot up from her chair.

'Please don't touch me.'

'Why not. Do you find me repulsive?'

Marianne refused to answer.

'She found me repulsive.'

Marianne didn't have to ask who.

He began to move around the kitchen, in and out of the shadows, large, malevolent. 'Love, devotion, that's not enough for some women, they must have constant excitement. He paused, bundled up the dress and threw it at her. 'Put it on.'

The dress caught Marianne full in the face and the scent of Felicity filled her nostrils. With a shudder of revulsion, she untangled herself and threw it to the ground. 'No!'

'Do as I say.'

'I – will – not.'

'Oh yes you will.' Grabbing Marianne he pushed her up against the wall, then, holding her with the weight of his body, and in spite of her struggles, he managed to pull the dress over her head. 'There.' He smiled a victor's smile, clamped her jaw between his thumb and forefinger and bent and kissed her. Suffocating, terrified, Marianne pummelled his chest and kicked out wildly.

Eventually he was forced to let go and Marianne spat in his face. He said nothing, wiped away the spittle with the back of his hand and then gave her a stinging slap on each cheek.

'Stop it!' she screamed. Gripped by a terrible dread that Felicity was about to take possession of her soul, she pulled obsessively at the fragile material, ripping at it with her fingernails until it hung on her in shreds.

'Think you've got the better of me, do you? But I must tell you that there's a wardrobe full of gowns upstairs.' Hugo Lacey held out his hand. 'Come, let me show you.'

'No.'

'Oh but you will.' He grabbed her wrist, unlocked the door, but as he dragged her into the hall, Marianne bent and sank her teeth into the back of his hand.

He swore vilely and his grip weakened, but although her legs threatened to buckle under her, Marianne managed to stumble up the stairs with no other thought than to escape this violent, crazy man.

Feeling her way along the landing, Marianne came to Mrs Lacey's old room and tried the handle. It was locked and he was behind her, holding the candlestick aloft. She tried to shrink into the fabric of the house but he moved forward until his face was close to hers and she could see his eyes, strange and wild. Acting with an animal instinct for survival, Marianne struck the candlestick out of his hand and it shattered on to the floor. Now in total darkness, she made to dodge past him, but he lifted her forcibly and carried her towards his bedroom.

'Boris, help me!' she screamed, in a last desperate bid to save herself, and miraculously the dog was there, hurling himself at Hugo and forcing him to let go. Hugo kicked out at him, but Boris grabbed a trouser leg and sank his teeth into Hugo's calf.

'Call the bastard off,' Hugo yelled, but Boris clung on, going in turns for his arms and face. It had now become a fight between man and dog and Marianne, barely rational herself, stood there clutching her head and screaming. She thought it was her crazed mind imagining the sound of wood splintering and glass breaking, until the beam from a torch was turned on her.

'Marianne?'

'Franz.' Sobbing, she ran along the landing.

Arms outstretched, blood running down his face, Hugo stumbled after her. 'Come back, Felicity my darling, my love, my life,' he pleaded, but Boris stood in his path, teeth bared. Backing away from him, Hugo leaned against the balustrade. Drunk, deranged, he cried out again, 'Felicity, my love, my life, don't leave me.' Then he swayed slightly, lost his balance, and with a cry and sickening thud, he somersaulted on to the tiled floor below.

Chapter Sixteen

I s ... is ... he dead?' Marianne's legs gave way and she was shaking so violently, she could barely speak.

'I do not know, but it is better if you do not look, *meine Liebling.*' Franz gathered her up and, talking to her softly in German and English, he carried Marianne down the stairs and into the kitchen.

'We must fetch the doctor, tell him what happened. The lorry is outside and the driver will take us to the village.' Franz wrapped his overcoat round her and helped Marianne into the lorry. He sat her next to the driver, who looked at her strangely but didn't say a word.

But shock had numbed her brain and she had no recollection of where the doctor's house was. In the end the driver was forced to stop and ask a villager the way, and as the man gave directions, he stared curiously at the dishevelled apparition in the lorry.

The doctor's wife was also taken aback to find a shabby POW and a hysterical young woman whom she vaguely recognized standing on her step. And the girl was dressed in the most incongruous get-up; a ragged garment which had once presumably been an evening dress and a man's overcoat. She was also babbling some nonsense about Hugo being dead.

'Captain Lacey ... could Doctor Gibb come please, it is very urgent,' said the young German. He was tense and pale and held the young woman protectively.

Beginning to get the sense that all was not well, Mrs Gibb held open the door.

'You'd better step inside for a moment while I fetch my husband.'

But the doctor was already walking through from the breakfast room at the back of the house. 'What is it, Daphne?'

'It's hard to get any sense out of this young woman. She says there's been an accident at Hope Grange. Hugo. I fear it's serious.'

Franz came forward. 'May I speak to you for a moment, Doctor?'

'Yes, come into my surgery.' The two men disappeared inside and without Franz's support, Marianne's legs gave way and she collapsed to the floor.

Mrs Gibb knelt down beside her. 'Why don't you come into the breakfast room, it's more comfortable in there,' she suggested, and held out both hands. Marianne grasped them, stumbled along the hall and into a scene of such domestic normality: a cat washing itself in front of the fire, two children in their nightclothes sipping a milky drink, that she was slightly calmed. Mrs Gibb had the good sense not to press her with questions, instead she brought her a thimbleful of brandy, which she insisted that Marianne should drink.

The children were sent up to bed, and a moment later, Doctor Gibb put his head round the door. 'Young Hartmann has given me some details, and I've spoken to Police Constable Barker. We're on our way now to Hope Grange to investigate. It's serious,' he added.

'What about this young lady?'

'Marianne, isn't it?' asked Doctor Gibb.

Marianne, who vaguely remembered that this was her name, nodded.

'She'd better stay here for the time being. When we get back PC Barker will probably want to ask her a few questions.'

Time lost all meaning for Marianne, but eventually Doctor Gibb returned and called to his wife. 'A word my dear.' Mrs Gibb glanced at Marianne then left the room. Some sort of discussion followed and when they returned a few minutes later they were accompanied by a policeman.

Doctor Gibb sat down beside her. 'Marianne, this is Police Constable Barker and he's going to ask you a few questions. Think you can manage that?'

Marianne nodded and the young policeman removed his helmet and took a small notepad and pencil from his top pocket. 'I know you're going to find it difficult, miss, so take your time, but I do need you to tell me how this tragedy at Hope Grange occurred.'

Marianne covered her face with her hands and her tears dripped through her fingers on to the dress. 'I ... I can't remember.'

Mrs Gibb went and put an arm round her shoulder. 'Can't we leave this until tomorrow, Constable?'

'I'm afraid not, Mrs G.' Police Constable Barker had never dealt with a death before, possibly a murder. He'd apprehended the odd poacher and the postman had had his bike nicked, but that hardly amounted to a crime wave, and this could mean promotion. 'Take your time, miss, start at the beginning,' he said, holding his pencil in readiness.

The beginning ... the beginning ... her voice as toneless as the speaking clock, Marianne began. 'He, Captain Lacey, told me the house was being sold and said I would have to look for another job. Then he got drunk and started throwing things – he did that a lot – so I decided to leave right away. But he locked the doors and forced me to put on this dress, I think it belonged to his wife ... and ... and ... he kissed me.' Too distressed to go on, Marianne drew in a great sobbing breath.

'And then?'

'I knew he'd gone mad ... so ... so ... I ran upstairs ... There was a power cut. He followed ... tried to force me into his bedroom, but Boris went for him. That's how I got away. He was calling for his wife and ... and lost his balance ...' The falling, falling, falling flashed before her eyes.

'Did you push him at any time.'

'Really Constable!' interjected Mrs Gibb.

'These questions have to be asked, Mrs Gibb, the cause of death established,' the bobby answered, somewhat defensively.

Marianne's head jerked up. 'Are you accusing me of killing him?'

'You might have pushed him without realizing it, while you were struggling to get free.'

'I was halfway down the stairs when he fell. Ask Franz if you don't believe me, he saw it all.'

'There might be more questions, but that will do for the time being,' said PC Barker, closing his notepad and returning it to his top pocket. It was clear from the girl's statement that the captain's mind had tipped over, but they'd always been a funny lot up at that house. 'You appreciate that there will have to be a post mortem and inquest?'

'We'll deal with that when the time comes,' said Doctor Gibb and saw him out. 'I think that's the worst of it over, my dear,' he said when he returned, 'although you and Franz will have to attend the inquest.'

Hardly knowing what an inquest was, the information didn't register with Marianne.

After this, Daphne Gibb, a capable woman who was used to dealing with emergencies, filled a hot-water bottle and made up the bed for Marianne in the spare bedroom. As she helped her undress, she took the precaution of removing the dress with the Worth label inside. Later, hiding it away in a bag under the stairs, she shook her head in despair that a young servant should find herself caught up in the maelstrom that was Hugo and Felicity.

They told Marianne later that she slept for twenty-four hours and that while she'd been asleep, Doctor Gibb had gone to the house and collected her suitcase and savings. With her own clothes and a bit of money, Marianne felt less dependent on the charity of the family, not that they made her feel like a penniless waif, quite the opposite. All of them, husband and wife, the children Rosalind and Tim, even the cat, showed her such kindness; she knew if it hadn't been for that sudden flash across her vision of a falling body, that cry, the sickening thud, she might have been able to get her life back to normal again.

It helped when, a few days later, Doctor Gibb brought Franz to see her, leaving them alone to talk. As soon as the door closed, Marianne threw herself in his arms. Franz kissed her gently, cherishing her and careful to rein in his passion until she was fully mended. 'I love you so much,' Franz murmured into her hair and with these words the healing process began.

Later they talked. 'If you hadn't turned up …' Marianne shivered. 'And Boris, he saved me. And where is the dear old dog?'

'At the camp with me and the chickens have a nice new home on Mr Thornton's farm. I was confined to camp, you know, for giving the captain a sock in the jaw.'

'A pity you didn't hit him harder. I wrote to the camp commandant telling him he'd called you a Nazi, but I don't expect it helped.'

'It did. As a serving officer, he said, the captain should have known better. I was let out early and I came right away to tell you my news.'

The news she'd been dreading. 'You're going home.' It was a statement.

Franz shook his head and smiled. 'No need for a long face. I think you will be a little bit pleased. I have been given permission to stay in England. I will have to work on the land for three years and Mr Thornton says I can work for him. But later I would like to go back to my studies, become a teacher like my father.'

'Oh Franz.' Unaccountably she started to cry.

'What's this? I thought my news would make you happy.' Franz laughed.

'It has, but I've often wondered whether I would ever see you again. And wait until I tell Gerald, he'll be over the moon.'

'Does he know that his father is dead?'

'He's gone to a convalescent home. Doctor Gibb is waiting until he's back to full health before he tells him.'

'Poor little fellow.'

'It's sad for him, but I've found out that his mother is alive.'

The mystery of Felicity's whereabouts had been revealed while she was drying up for Mrs Gibb one morning after breakfast. The subject of Gerald came up and Marianne wondered aloud where he might go and live.

Thinking to herself *not here I hope*, Mrs Gibb tipped the tea leaves from the pot into a basin to dry. Later they would go on the fire. 'That I don't know. It's such a tragic mess, though there is his mother.'

'Where is she?'

'In the county asylum.'

Marianne nearly dropped the plate she was drying. 'The asylum?'

'Private wing,' Mrs Gibb added, as if this helped.

'The butcher told me she ran off with another man.'

'Yes she did, the silly girl. But her mind was quite broken when her lover was shot down over Germany and she was left destitute in a couple of rooms without even the money to pay the rent. He'd also neglected to tell her that he already had a wife. Shortly after that she gave birth to a stillborn baby. She and Hugo had already lost their first-born, little Hugo, to measles and she was quite fragile mentally for some time after that, but appeared to recover.'

'If she couldn't pay the rent, why didn't she get a job?' Marianne asked getting down to practicalities.

'Women of Felicity's class don't work.'

'Did you know her well?'

'My husband is a humble GP, so we weren't part of their set, but occasionally, if they were short of a couple, they would invite us up to play bridge. That's how well I knew her.'

'What was she like as a person?'

'Charming, self-centred. An excess of charm always bothers me. Don't think I'm excusing in any way what Hugo did to you, my dear, and those hours of terror he subjected you to, but some of the blame must be laid at Felicity's door. Hugo did adore her, but he also wanted to control her, which was difficult with her will-o'-the-wisp temperament. Unfortunately she was also susceptible to flattery and it goes without saying that she loved parties, hunting and balls and thought that money grew on trees. But the good times came to a halt when war was declared and Hugo joined up. There she was, cooped up at Hope Grange with old Mrs Lacey, a small child, nothing but shortages and all the fun gone out of her life. Then along comes a dashing young bomber pilot and the chance of some excitement.'

Marianne remembered the letter, the assignations in the stables where she must have betrayed her wedding vows, and blushed.

'It's common knowledge that the family's been living on credit for years and then there was the expense of keeping Felicity in the private wing. No wonder Hugo's creditors were chasing him. And Hope Grange meant so much to him. It was bound up with his pride and the family name. I think he broke under the shame of losing it.'

Marianne hoped she wasn't supposed to feel sorry for him. 'He never took Gerald to see his mother, you know.'

'Perhaps she was too ill at the time.'

That was giving Hugo the benefit of the doubt. She knew better than anyone what he was capable of. Out of spite, he would have denied his wife the right to see her child. In fact it wasn't beyond him to have had Felicity committed to a mental institution for daring to be unfaithful to him, a Lacey, of long and illustrious lineage.

'So, as you can see, a lot of lives have been ruined because passion was put before common sense.'

'Do you think his mother will ever be able to look after Gerald?'

'It would certainly solve a lot of problems, but it depends on what sort of shape Felicity is in mentally. There might be a bit of money left once the sale of Hope Grange has gone through and the debts are settled. And I imagine they'll be entitled to one of the council houses, once they're built, although council houses aren't quite Felicity's thing.'

'And if she can't look after him?'

Mrs Gibb shrugged. 'Relatives, if there are any; otherwise an orphanage.'

'But that can't happen.'

Mrs Gibb glanced at her. 'What do you propose then, my dear?'

'I ... I don't know ...' Marianne answered, but she knew Gerald would go to an orphanage over her dead body.

Mrs Gibb emptied the washing-up bowl, and while she was stacking away the cups and saucers and plates, she said to Marianne, 'Do you think you could keep an eye on things here while I go and visit a friend who's none too well?'

''Course, I can,' answered Marianne, who was anxious to earn her keep.

Mrs Gibb went and fetched her hat and coat. 'I won't be long and it's quite straightforward. If someone comes to the door asking to see my husband, tell them there will be a surgery tonight at six. If the phone rings, take a message. There's a pad and pencil by the phone. Think you can you manage that?'

'I'm sure I can.' And she did, just about, because from the moment Mrs Gibb stepped out of the house, neither the doorbell, nor the phone stopped ringing. Patients who came to the door were easy to deal with: 'Come back at six,' but the telephone calls tried Marianne's patience to the limit. Invariably they came from a phone box, often from people nervous about using a phone and who didn't realize they had to press button A before they could speak. Then halfway through taking down the patient's name and address, the money would run out and the caller would be cut off. One woman even expected her to diagnose her husband's illness and got quite nasty when Marianne explained that she couldn't.

Although Mrs Gibb was a trained nurse, as Marianne replaced the receiver for the umpteenth time, she wondered how she coped with the constant interruptions while looking after her family and helping her husband in the surgery. *And now she has me, an extra burden.* But she couldn't continue indefinitely to rely on the family's good will. However, while she looked for a job, she would do her best to make herself useful.

The front bell buzzed. More sick people. Well, at least their problems take my mind off the inquest, thought Marianne, and went to answer it.

But as things do, the day eventually came. Marianne was all on edge as Doctor Gibb drove her and Franz to the coroner's court, and not even his reassurances helped. 'Now remember, you are not on trial; all you have to do is answer a few questions.' As it turned out he was right, the coroner questioned her, Franz, PC Barker and the doctor, listened to their answers and at the end gave a verdict of death by misadventure.

Marianne heard the verdict and a cloud lifted. At last she was freed from the burden of Hugo Lacey's death. Holding hands, she and Franz walked out into the spring sunshine. Now they could get on with their lives, in spite of the funeral still to come. Not that Marianne had any intention of mourning Hugo Lacey's passing.

'I shan't be going to the funeral,' she told Franz later, when the arrangements had been completed. 'But Gerald will be there, so will you give him my love? I really worry about what's to become of him.'

'Mr Thornton has a small cottage on his farm, it is empty and he has told me I can have it when I leave the camp. But I have no furniture. If we collect the beds from Hope Grange and what's left of the furniture, Gerald could come and stay with me until his mother is well and the council houses are built.'

'You are a clever, lovely man,' Marianne said and kissed him. 'But how do we get the furniture out to the farm?'

'On the pick-up lorry.'

'I'll speak to Doctor Gibb, see what he thinks.'

The doctor, who had been worrying that he might have to inflict another orphan on his long-suffering wife, thought it a brilliant idea. 'We'll have to hurry, the bulldozers will be moving in soon.'

'Should we take Gerald to have one last look at the house?'

Roger Gibb shook his head. 'It might upset him. Let's get all the stuff over to the cottage so that when he leaves the convalescent home he can move straight in with Franz. He'll be so ecstatic about being reunited with Boris he won't give a thought to the house being demolished.'

There followed some frantic activity for the next week or so. Marianne went over with Franz to check the cottage. It was pretty basic, with no electricity and an outside toilet. But the slate roof looked sound and there was no sign of damp. Downstairs consisted of a parlour, a scullery and wash-house; upstairs there were two small bedrooms. It would do, Marianne decided, after the cobwebs had been knocked down, the windows cleaned and the wall given a going over with a couple of pots of distemper.

Next Franz nabbed Pete, the good-natured driver, and he drove them over to Hope Grange. As they approached, Marianne's spine began to tingle, her palms to sweat. It looked even more forbidding than that first time she'd set eyes on it. As far as she was concerned, the sooner it was flattened the better. If she'd known what she was letting herself that first evening as she followed Gerald up the drive, she'd have turned tail. She glanced at Franz. And she would not have met the love of her life. She leaned her head on his shoulder and he put an arm around her and kissed her.

'I know what you are thinking, but do not be frightened. I am here. I will always be here.'

The lorry stopped by the back door, but even Franz's reassuring presence couldn't prevent Marianne's hand from shaking as she inserted the key in the lock. The door creaked open and she smelt blood and death. She shuddered and stepped back.

'I can't go in, I'm sorry.'

'I understand. We'll get the stuff out.'

'There's a wicker basket in the attic with a lot of photograph albums in it; it's important you rescue that, Franz, for Gerald's sake.'

It was the first thing Franz and the driver brought down. Then, deciding it would fit nicely into the cottage, he went back and collected the rocking-chair.

While she was waiting Marianne went and got the bike from the stables. She stood for a moment, listening, but the ghosts of two lovers, the horses and their riders, had sensibly fled, taking their unhappiness with them.

She wandered round the derelict garden, but the atmosphere

soon depressed her and she hurried back to the house to find that a carpet, blankets, sheets, two single beds, the kitchen table and chairs, had already been loaded on to the lorry.

'I'm glad you left the sofa behind,' she said to Franz.

'I had to, it was full of woodworm.'

Yes, thought Marianne, and dark memories, too.

Space was found for the bike and they set off down the drive. It was growing dark but Marianne didn't look back and she knew she wouldn't return here until council houses with bathrooms and hot and cold running water had finally laid the ghosts and obliterated the past.

Chapter Seventeen

Mrs Gibb and Marianne had come to an arrangement: until she found a job, and she was looking, for ten shillings a week and her keep she would help out around the house. Marianne was so grateful to the family for taking her in that she would have gladly worked for them for nothing, but Mrs Gibb insisted on a fair wage. As she pointed out, it put things on a more businesslike footing, and made her feel less awkward about asking Marianne to take on more responsible tasks.

Displaying a faith in her cooking that Marianne hoped she could justify, this morning Mrs Gibb had gone out shopping and left her to prepare a meat pie for dinner. Her hands were submerged in fat and flour when the front doorbell went.

A patient. *Couldn't have timed it better*, she grumbled *sotto voce* to the figure outlined in the glass panel of the door.

'Yes, can I help you?' Marianne wiped her hands on her apron in a way that suggested she was being greatly inconvenienced by the interruption.

'I do hope so, duckie,' the smartly dressed woman standing on the step chirped.

Marianne did a double take, then her face lit up with joy. 'Renée!' she screamed, and forgetting her floury hands gave her aunt a great big hug. 'When did you get here? Are you staying?' The questions poured from her lips.

'Do I have to stand on the step or can I come in?'

'It's not my house, but seeing you're my aunt, I don't suppose Mrs Gibb will mind,' said Marianne, and led her into the kitchen.

'Now let me have a good look at you.' Marianne was silent while she studied her aunt, coveting her Cossack-style coat with its astrakhan collar and matching hat. After some moments she delivered her judgement. 'My, you do look posh.'

'Knowing clothes are still rationed here, I made sure I kitted myself out before I left New York. I've got a few things for you, as well. A pretty dress you'll love.'

'I still can't believe it. I'd given up hope of ever seeing you again.'

'Now why should you do that, when I told you I was coming home?'

'Yes, and then you went off to Florida, and it's ages since I heard from you.'

'I did write, lovie, I swear.' Renée sat down and looked about her. 'Comfy house,' she observed. 'Bit different from that great mausoleum.'

'Have you been up to Hope Grange?'

'An extravagance, I guess, but I got a taxi from Leicester and went straight there. And what do I find? This weird house, and not a soul living in it. Gave me the creeps, I can tell you. I told the taxi driver to get the hell out of it before Count Dracula jumped out from behind a bush and sank his fangs into my neck. Not knowing what had happened to you, sweetheart, really bothered me, I can tell you. The taxi driver dropped me off at the pub. I think he was in a hurry to get back to civilization. But I took a risk and booked in for a couple of nights. I heard your terrible story from the publican. Oh, my pet, what you've been through.' Renée's eyes grew moist as she stood up and wrapped her arms around her niece.

'You heard their version of events. It's behind me now and I'm trying to forget it, but when I can face it again without having nightmares, I'll tell you the full, correct story, not village gossip. Anyway, having you home makes me feel better already.' Marianne kissed her aunt affectionately. 'Promise me you won't go off and leave me again?'

'Never ever. Biggest mistake of my life marrying Chuck, and I had the bruises to prove it. Tell you what, though, after Florida, England's bleedin' freezing.'

'It's been a long hard winter, but spring's around the corner.'

'Well, it had better hurry. And I'll have to start looking for a job soon, the money's running low.'

'You won't have any trouble finding one, there are heaps of vacancies and you seem to be able to walk into any job you like.'

'I might go back to being a telephonist. How do you fancy coming to London and us finding a room together?'

'Sorry, I can't. You see, I've met someone,' Marianne said awkwardly.

'Can't say I'm surprised, you're quite a looker, and so like your mum. Local lad, is he?'

Marianne shuffled her feet and blushed. There was no easy way of telling her aunt. 'No ... he's ...'

'Spit it out.'

'His name is Franz and he's a German prisoner of war,' she said in a rush.

'A German? You can't love a German, it's impossible, not after they murdered my mum and half the street.'

'Yes I can. Franz didn't kill anyone. He was a prisoner of war in America most of the time.'

Renée stood up. 'I'm sorry, love, but you've given me a nasty shock and I need time to think it over, so I'm going now.'

Marianne fumbled in the sleeve of her jumper for her hand-kerchief. 'I love Franz, but I love you too, and you promised you'd never leave me again,' she sobbed.

At that precise moment Mrs Gibb walked into the kitchen with her shopping, saw a strange woman standing there, a half-made pie on the table and Marianne crying into her handkerchief.

Glancing from one to the other, she asked, 'May I ask what is going on?'

Renée held out her hand. 'Mary ... Marianne might have mentioned me, I'm her aunt, Mrs Zuckerman, and I've just arrived back from America.'

Mrs Gibb placed her shopping basket on the table. 'But why the tears? You've been longing to see your aunt.'

Marianne blew her nose and left it to Renée to explain.

'It's this German ... of all the men in the world to fall in love with...' Renée was lost for words.

'I understand your feelings, of course I do, Mrs Zuckerman, but with the help of the church, what we are trying to do around here is proceed in an atmosphere of forgiveness. It is the only way forward and Franz is a gentle and kind young man, who clearly loves your niece deeply.'

'I'm sure he does.'

'Look, why don't you come back at four,' Mrs Gibb suggested as she showed Renée out, 'and we'll sit down together and discuss it over a cup of tea. And may I say,' she added in an undertone, 'that if Franz hadn't turned up that night at Hope Grange, I shudder to think what might have happened to Marianne.'

A scattering of crumbs on the tablecloth was all that remained of the meat pie, the children had returned to school, Doctor Gibb was out on his rounds, Mrs Gibb was upstairs repairing sheets on her treadle sewing-machine, the cat was giving herself a pedicure and Marianne was washing the pots. She was scouring out a saucepan when the phone rang.

'Can you answer it please, Marianne?' Mrs Gibb called down.

'On my way,' Marianne replied, and was astonished to hear Franz's voice on the other end of the line.

'Marianne, I have left the camp for the last time. After five years I am a free man and I am so happy. I will go now straight to the cottage and sing all the way there.'

'Don't go yet. Wait for me; I'll come and meet you.' She replaced the phone and ran up the stairs to the sewing room.

'Franz has been released from the camp. Is it all right if I cycle out to meet him and bring him back here, so that he can meet Renée?'

'Won't it be a bit awkward for Franz? I thought we decided that the three of us were going to talk it over first?'

'There's nothing to discuss. I'm not giving up Franz. If it's going to cause a rift between my aunt and me I'm sorry, but nothing will make me change my mind. I can't remember Renée asking for my permission when she married Chuck and went off to America, and I was pretty upset at the time. And if she'd stayed there she wouldn't have cared two hoots that I had a German boyfriend.'

'You have a point there.'

'So can I bring him back, Mrs Gibb?'

'If that's what you want, but you'd better prepare him for her hostility.'

'Franz has been a prisoner of war for five years, he's used to hostility and I don't expect Renée will spit at him, like some have.'

'As long as he knows. Your aunt doesn't look the sort of woman who minces her words.'

'I'll warn him, don't worry.' In a rush of excitement, Marianne tore down the stairs, pulled the bike from the garden shed and pedalled like mad out to the camp. The lane twisted and turned like a stick of barley sugar and now that the snow was at last melting it was full of potholes and puddles, and a viscous sludge sprayed out from either side of the wheels of the bike, coating Marianne's legs in mud. Hardly at my best to meet Franz, she thought, turned a corner and there he was, his step jaunty, head held high, the creases in his shabby uniform razor sharp and with a small wooden case containing his few possessions swinging in his hand.

When he saw her he opened his arms wide and shouted to the sky, 'I am a free man. A free man!' Laughing, Marianne flung down the bike and ran to him. Franz scooped her up and swung her round. 'I'm free! I'm free!' he repeated and began to kiss her with a hungry passion. With a quickening heartbeat, Marianne responded eagerly. 'Oh, Marianne, I do love you so,' Franz murmured and started to unbutton the front of her dress. Marianne had a moment's doubt. Should a good girl allow this? she wondered, but when he pulled down her shoulder strap and began kissing the rise of her breasts, she succumbed with a guilty pleasure.

'Disgoostin'!' a voice shouted.

With flushed faces they leapt guiltily apart. Then they saw that it was the old peddler who went around the area on his horse and cart mending chairs and sharpening knives. His lecherous eyes went from Franz's uniform to Marianne, who was valiantly trying to hold her dress together. 'Whore!' he snarled, then spat on the ground.

'How dare you!' Franz made a lunge at the old man, but seeing it coming, Marianne grabbed his arm. 'Don't Franz, please. There'll be trouble.'

'Yeah, trouble,' the peddler babbled.

'I don't care; he insulted you.' Franz flexed his fingers, barely able to stem his anger.

'He's old and a bit simple.'

But not so stupid he'd hang around for a punch in the guts. Whacking his horse into a trot, the peddler wisely got the hell out of it.

'Peeping Tom,' Franz shouted after him, then he picked up

the bike and they walked on. But his earlier carefree manner had vanished; now his shoulders were hunched, his expression bleak. Marianne shook his hand. 'Franz, try not to let it affect you.'

He stopped and stared down at her. 'How can I, a German, one of the enemy, ask you to marry me? Insults like this will happen all the time and it could destroy the love we have for each other.'

'Had you thought of asking me, then?' Marianne ventured.

'Yes.'

'Well, go on. Do it.'

Franz took her hand. 'Marianne, will you be my wife?' He looked so solemn, she got a fit of the giggles.

'Why do you laugh?'

'Because I love you.'

'So what is your answer?'

'Yes, yes a hundred times yes.'

'Even though I have nothing?'

'You've given me your love, that's all that matters.' She kissed him again to reassure him.

'Oh, Marianne, I am so happy to have you. As soon as it is allowed we will be husband and wife and I will cherish you and care for you until my dying day, that is my promise to you.'

'There is one hurdle. My Aunt Renée's back from America and not exactly over the moon about me and you. When she hears we're getting married, she might try and prevent it. But once I'm twenty-one I can marry whoever I wish.'

'We will wait then.'

'Do you feel up to meeting her?'

Franz straightened his shoulders and looked resolute. 'I am ready for it.'

Mrs Gibb spoke in a refined sort of way, Renée's accent was pure South London, peppered with a few Americanisms and Marianne could hear them chatting as she opened the door. Pulling a reluctant Franz forward, she said in a defiant voice, 'Renée, this is Franz, and we've got some news for you. We're to be married.'

She'd geared herself up for growls of outrage, so she was unprepared for the smiling faces and Renée walking towards them, holding out her hand to Franz. 'Congratulations, Franz, and I don't suppose you need me to tell you that my niece is a rather special young woman.'

Franz put his arm round Marianne's shoulder and gazed down at her with a tender smile. 'She is certainly very special to me.'

Renée's face softened and any last residue of hostility melted away. Taking Marianne aside Mrs Gibb said quietly, 'We had a long chat while you were out and your aunt accepts that love doesn't pay much attention to boundaries and race. Now come and sit down, the pair of you, and we'll drink a toast. I think there's some British sherry left over from Christmas.' She rummaged around in the sideboard and brought out a bottle and glasses. And so bridges were built. A couple of glasses of sherry later, Renée had her hand on Franz's knee and was telling him that he was the politest, most charming man she'd ever met, adding with a wink, 'and young Marianne here ought to watch out.'

The next day Marianne saw her aunt on to the bus for Leicester. A week later Renée phoned to tell her she'd found herself a bedsit in a leafy area called Stoneygate and employment as a receptionist/telephonist in a solicitor's office in town. 'Oh and by the way, I've got myself a new chap. Met him at a dance. Goes by the name of Desmond. I'll introduce you sometime.'

Chapter Eighteen

Pretty soon Gerald would be arriving with Dr Gibb. After a great deal of hard work the house was now spotless. Floors had been scrubbed to within an inch of their lives, cobwebs swept away, walls distempered and the mice sent packing. Mrs Gibb had kindly made them curtains for the parlour, and Marianne and Franz had just finished threading them with string before hanging them at the window. Some threadbare carpets that even Hugo Lacey hadn't managed to flog, kept out the worst of the draughts, and the rocking-chair had already been commandeered by one of the farm cats.

Arms wrapped round each other, they stood admiring the room and agreeing that they were indeed fortunate to have this cottage when so many families were homeless or on waiting lists.

Marianne could sometimes get through a whole day now without experiencing flashbacks and reliving that terrifying night when Hugo Lacey finally went off his head and became so completely deranged she thought it was all up for her.

But she had survived. In fact she felt so blessed these days she knew it was in her own interest to concentrate on all the good things in her life, to try and banish anything dark. She had Franz, and Renée home for good, she hoped, and although she and Franz could only afford the basic necessities, she felt that, between them, they'd already changed the cottage into a real home.

'What this house needs now is many, many children,' said Franz.

Marianne smiled up at him. 'How many?'

'Six.'

Briefly across Marianne's vision there flitted six sun-blond versions of Franz, but then her practical side took over. There would be no children without marriage. 'Oh Franz, how long do you think we'll have to wait before we get permission to marry?'

'You can never tell, but it will be soon, I hope. It is better that I do not keep asking, because they are getting annoyed with me, I think. We have to try and be patient and enjoy what we have, which is quite a lot. Also Gerald needs time to settle in.'

'And that reminds me, I'd better put the kettle on for our first guests.' While she was setting out cups and saucers and a home-made cake, Marianne heard a car's hooter outside.

'That'll be them,' said Franz and, drawing Marianne's arm through his, they went to welcome Gerald to his new home.

Dr Gibb had been to collect Gerald from the nursing home and as he stepped down from the doctor's car, Marianne was shocked at how fragile he looked. 'My Lord, he's just skin and bones, and look how pale and pinched his face is,' she exclaimed as he ran towards them on matchstick legs.

'Supposing Gerald does not like living here with me,' said Franz, voicing a doubt he'd so far kept to himself.

'You'll be giving him the love he craved from his father, but never got, and don't forget you're also giving him a home. He could have ended up in an orphanage, and after Hope Grange, with its leaks and broken windows, always cold, always damp, our little home will seem like Buckingham Palace. But he can play up, so he does need a firm hand,' Marianne warned.

'We must also remember that he has lost his father.'

'He'll be grieving for him, of course.'

'Yes. Captain Lacey had many troubles.'

'Please don't feel sorry for him, he was evil,' Marianne said sharply and pulled away from Franz.

He was cursing himself for his thoughtlessness, when Gerald reached them and stopped, paralyzed by a sudden shyness.

'Hello Gerald,' said Marianne.

'Hello,' he mumbled, staring at his shoes with unusual interest.

'Are you better?'

He nodded.

'Don't I get a kiss, then?' She held out her arms and he flung himself at her.

'Am I really going to stay here with Franz?' he asked.

'You certainly are, young man,' Franz answered, and picking him up, he swung him round. 'And we'll be putting some flesh back on those bones, Marianne's cooking will see to that because, right now, I could play a tune on those ribs of yours.'

The sound of Gerald's voice had woken Boris from his slumbers and he came bounding out, hurling himself at his old companion with such boundless joy that Gerald stumbled and fell. Soon they were a jumble of legs, arms and slobbery kisses.

Marianne turned to Doctor Gibb, who was looking on with an indulgent smile. 'Is all this excitement good for him? And should he be rolling around on the ground?'

'Can't do much harm. Poor little blighter's had a tough time of it lately, so what he needs right now is to do all the things boys of his age do and for his life to be as normal as possible.'

Stifling the urge to cluck like a mother hen, Marianne waited for Gerald to exhaust himself with Boris, then she held out her hand. 'Come on, I'll show you your bedroom.'

As they approached the house, he stopped. 'Is this where I'm going to live?'

'It is.'

'It is rather small.'

Marianne suppressed a smile. 'So are you, young man, so you

should fit in nicely. And wait until you see your bedroom, it's even smaller.'

She'd tried to make his bedroom look as much like his old one as possible and she waited for his comments on this.

As if to get his bearings, Gerald went and touched a few familiar objects: his books, the sailing ship Franz had made him, the Bible his grandmother had given him, the Meccano set; his father's last present to him. 'Is it because my father's dead that they're pulling down Hope Grange?'

'No, dear. Your father had decided to sell it before that. It was a big house and there wasn't the money to maintain it. But they're going to build new houses on the land and eventually you'll be able to live in one of them with your mother.'

'If you don't mind, I'd prefer to stay here with Franz and Boris,' he replied and went back downstairs.

Later, driving home with Doctor Gibb, Marianne repeated this worrying conversation.

'It's not surprising. It's such a long time since Gerald saw his mother she'll be almost a stranger to him. They'll have to get reacquainted, and that won't be easy for either of them.'

'How did she seem?'

'She is in no way insane, only institutionalized. She knows Hugo is dead, but she bore her grief well.'

Remembering how she'd once been obsessed with Felicity, Marianne couldn't help asking, 'Is she still beautiful?'

Dr Gibb thought. 'She was so stunning when she was young it almost took your breath away. She isn't now, and her dark hair is turning grey but she still has wonderful cheekbones.'

'Maybe she'll marry again.'

'Her charm is still intact, so she might at that, but her husband will need money, because what did distress her, more than anything, was learning that Hope Grange is soon to be demolished. She wanted to know why, and couldn't grasp the concept of money running out. She wasn't over the moon at the idea of living in a council house, I'll tell you, but since the choice is that or remaining in the asylum, and she's no longer in the private wing, I think she'll settle for the council house. Lord knows how she'll cope; she's never lifted a finger in her life. But we'll deal with that problem as it arises.'

'If she's better, why did he keep her in there?'

'One word: control. When she eloped and lost her lover and his baby, she had a complete breakdown. That was why she was in the asylum in the first place. But when she recovered Hugo kept her there, for outside he could never be one hundred per cent sure where she was or what she was up to.'

'That was wicked, and if you ask me, it was Hugo Lacey who should have been locked up, not his wife, because he *clearly* was mad,' Marianne responded with some bitterness.

Dr Gibb gave her a sideways glance. 'I know. I'm sorry, my dear, for mentioning his name, but I forget sometimes. You've coped so well.'

'During the day, yes, but not in the small hours, when I wake in a sweat and it all comes back He was completely off his head, you know, and he was going to going lock me in the cellar and leave me there. And he would have raped me, you know, and then he would have murdered me. He thought I was Felicity. If it hadn't been for Boris and Franz ...' Marianne began to sob quietly and Dr Gibbs patted her hand.

'I'm glad you've been able to talk to me about it, my dear, it does help, and I could arrange for you to see a professional at the hospital so that you can talk about these nightmares.'

Marianne gave him a suspicious look. 'Do you mean one of those head doctors? No thanks, I'll get over it in time. All I want now is for Franz and me to be married, that will make everything better.'

Dr Gibb smiled. 'Good girl, let's hope it's soon.'

*

On the following Sunday, Renée caught the bus out to Stretton Magna to meet Gerald, view the transformed cottage and have dinner with Marianne and Franz.

The farmer and his wife had very generously provided them with eggs, milk, and a succulent joint of beef, and Marianne's Yorkshire pudding rose like a barrage balloon. As part of her campaign to fatten Gerald up, for afters she'd made steamed syrup pudding and custard.

'That was scrumptious,' said Gerald, as he and Franz held out their plates for seconds. 'They used to give us jam roly-poly in hospital and some of the patients called it dead man's leg.' He screwed up his nose. 'It put me right off.'

'It's better than we got in the camp, too,' Franz added.

Marianne laughed. 'I should hope so; only the best ingredients are used in this house. Renée, what about you?'

'It was lovely, dear, but I've got to watch this.' Renée patted her waistline.

After that no one could move so they settled around the fire while Renée told them about her job in the solicitor's office, her bedsit and her new boyfriend. Desmond had gone, to be replaced by Len.

This is my family, Marianne thought, small but select, although Gerald was only on loan, because Hope Grange was in the process of being flattened, and the lake had already been filled in. She'd heard as well that the new development was to be called Hope Grange Estate and that the rusting gates had gone to the blacksmith to be repaired, after which they would be erected in an honoured position at the entrance to the estate.

A Sunday afternoon inertia had now fallen on the room, but then Franz startled everyone by jumping to his feet. 'If I don't get some exercise I will fall asleep. Come Boris, we will go for a walk.'

'Wait for me, I'm, coming too,' said Gerald, and went and fetched his coat.

When they'd gone, Renée sat up. 'I'm glad we've got some time alone, because now that you're marrying and are likely to have kids of your own, it's right that you should know something about your dad.'

'This is a bit sudden. I wasn't even sure he was alive.'

'He's alive all right. I've wanted to talk to you about him for a long time, but you know how your Nan was: called him for everything, blamed him for everything.'

'Yes, "that rotter" was one of Nan's milder expressions.'

'He's not the bounder Ma made him out to be, but she took against him for many reasons, not all of them Jonny's fault, although there's no getting away from he fact that he did get Sylvie, your mum, in the family way. But I'd better start at the beginning so you'll understand how all this bitterness came about. I expect you know that my dad was gassed in the Great War.'

Remembering the photograph of a moustachioed soldier on her grandmother's sideboard, Marianne nodded.

'Poor Dad, he was never fit enough to work again and by 1920 he was dead. Ma was left with two small girls and no money except her widow's pension, which wouldn't keep a sparrow alive. If she worked, she lost it, so we were on our uppers.

'A couple of streets away there was this family by the name of Ellis.'

Marianne sat up. 'Did you say Ellis?'

'That's right. Husband and wife and loads of kids. Things like marriage vows didn't mean much to Dave Ellis, especially when his eyes alighted on your grandmother, who was quite a looker in her time. She was also lonely, he was a charmer and the inevitable happened. Dave was a small-time crook and Nan soon got drawn into his various schemes.'

'Are you saying that my grandmother became a criminal?'

'I wouldn't put it as crudely as that. Yer Nan went in for a bit of shoplifting, but she was one of the best in the trade and never got caught,' said Renée with simple pride.

'Oh my God, if Franz hears about this he'll never marry me!'

'Don't get all high and mighty, love, you wouldn't have been dressed so pretty or lived so well. And it was a question of survival, because the twenties were bloody hard.'

Too agitated to sit still, Marianne began pacing the room. 'I remember when I was a kid going to Selfridges with her. She came out with this fox fur draped round her neck. I suppose she lifted that?'

'Probably. I must say I'm a bit surprised she involved you. Anyway, it didn't last with her and Dave. He found another woman and dumped yer Nan. She went to pieces. I remember how Sylvie and me used to stand outside her bedroom door every night and her sobs would break yer heart. Then one night they stopped. There were no more blokes and after that she concentrated on her business interests. A few years passed, by which time Sylvie was nearly sixteen and a real stunner. And then didn't history go and repeat itself and she fell hook, line and sinker for Jonny Ellis, Dave's eldest boy. Mind you, she had to join a queue, because the girls were like bees round a honeypot; a tall, dark, handsome honey pot. But your mother was determined and she pursued him single-mindedly and eventually she hooked him. And he didn't rape her like yer Nan used to make out, she was absolutely besotted. My mum would have locked her up and thrown away the key if she'd known she was seeing an Ellis so the fibs just flew out of Sylvie's rosebud mouth. She would make out she was taking me to the pictures, dump me in some fleapit and collect me a couple of hours later. I saw all the Charlie Chaplin films twice over. Then she fell pregnant with you, was too frightened to tell our mum and kept it hidden for five months before our mum found out, and by then it was too late to do anything about it.'

'I know that if Mum had had a gun she would have killed Jonny. And then my darling sister died.' Renée paused for a moment to compose herself. 'Jonny was banned from the funeral, banned from seeing you, his daughter. End of story.'

'I don't think it is.' Sensing this was a life-changing moment Marianne went over to the wicker basket and pulled out the sketchbook. Sitting down next to Renée, she opened it.

'They're pretty,' said Renée, admiring the faded watercolours.

'Never mind the paintings, this is what I want to show you. There's stuff written in this book that will give you the shock of your life and is such a coincidence, you're going to find it hard to believe.' As she turned the pages, Marianne filled Renée in on the dark history of the Laceys, and Anna, Jack and Barbara. 'Barbara is the one whose sketchbook this is. Listen to what she has written. *I know people are saying that I have done well for myself and I have and I am glad. Felix is fully returned to health and tomorrow I shall be Mrs Felix Lacey, for which I thank God.* The handwriting was firm, the tone jubilant.

Marianne stopped reading and looked up. 'Want to hear any more?'

'If you like.'

Marianne turned over a few pages and here the handwriting had deteriorated into an unsteady, tear-stained smudge; it was obvious that the writer was in a state of some distress. '*Such a terrible tragedy has befallen this family and although my hand shakes at I write I must put it all down,*' read Marianne. '*That Jack Ellis … Anna, my cousin … how could she…*'

Renée sat up.

'Anna was her cousin, and she stole the family jewels from Barbara on her wedding day,' Marianne explained. 'On that same day Jack Ellis ended Hugo Lacey's life by striking him with a metal bar. The poacher's stories vary but according to one version, Hugo had Anna pinned to the ground with one hand round her throat and was raping her most violently.'

'Good God! And you believe that Jack Ellis is one of your dad's ancestors? But Ellis is a common enough name and it could be anyone. What happened after that?'

'Jack was caught and hanged. Anna died in childbirth in some lodging house in Camberwell and lies in a pauper's grave.' Marianne's head suddenly jerked up and a look of horror spread across her face. 'It's just occurred to me: that child could have been Hugo's.'

'But you don't even know whether the infant survived. Its chances were pretty slim without his mother's milk. But one thing is certain in this life, ducky, we sure as hell can't choose our ancestors. So you reckon that Anna's child didn't die and that your dad is descended from either this Jack Ellis or Hugo Lacey? She must have been a pretty stupid, this Anna, if she thought she could get away with a robbery on that scale.'

'Supposing I've got their bad blood in me?'

'Don't be so melodramatic. We've all probably got dodgy ancestors, so let it go and get on with your life. Think of what you have and be grateful. What happened a hundred years ago is no fault of yours.'

'Well, I expect that this man, who might be my dad, is a crook like the rest of his family.'

'He works in a bank actually.'

'What, robbing it?'

'Don't be cynical, dear. He had the sense to cut himself off from his family. He married a nice girl, but she was consumptive and died during the war. I've been in touch with him since I got back; you're his only child and he's desperate to meet you.'

'I don't know; there's so much to take in and I'm that confused my head's buzzing. I'll have to talk it over with Franz first.'

*

The following day, on her way to the butcher's, Marianne took a detour through the graveyard. Pausing at the headstone of the murdered Hugo Lacey, she wondered at the strange coincidence that had brought her to Stretton Magna to work for the Lacey family, then to have history so eerily repeat itself. And knowing what she did now, the inscription on the headstone puzzled her. *Cut down by a woman in the full flower of his manhood.* Yet the family knew it was Jack who had killed Hugo, not Anna. *The debt he owed was small to cost him his life.* The debt being Hugo's rape of Anna, she supposed, brushed off as a trifling matter. Anna was wicked, she accepted that, but she hadn't murdered Hugo. The family distorted the truth to take revenge on Anna and so, each November, Anna, her great-great-grandmother was sacrificed on a bonfire for a murder she hadn't commited. Well not for much longer, because she was going to speak to Mr Veal about it, tell him the true story and see that Anna was spared that yearly humiliation. Marianne turned away. It was time to be done with the past and to meet her father.

Chapter Nineteen

As soon as the authorities gave their permission, Marianne and Franz went to see the vicar and set the date for their wedding. Franz bought a second-hand suit, his first since before the war and which, he assured Marianne, would look good as new once he'd given it a good brush and a press with a damp cloth. Marianne was more fortunate; her wedding dress had come all the way from America. It was cotton with a pattern of small blue flowers on a white background and, with its heart-shaped neck, was in her opinion very, very Hollywood. A small veil was kept in place with a garland of summer flowers made by Mrs Gibb. Renée, who was already familiar with most of the shops in Leicester, went with her to choose some shoes that would go with her dress and, after much indecision, she eventually settled on sandals in two shades of cream with lots of straps and heels that were higher than she was used to.

'How do I look?' she asked her audience.

Renée smiled. 'A right bobby-dazzler.'

'Beautiful,' added Mrs Gibb. She handed Marianne a posy made up of carnations, lavender and roses, picked from her garden less than half an hour ago and tied together with a blue satin ribbon that matched her dress.

Fighting off an attack of nerves, Marianne turned to her aunt, 'The wedding's at three. If my father's giving me away, shouldn't he be here by now?'

'Stop panicking. He was thrilled to be asked, so do you think he would let you down on this of all days? A fine start that would be.'

'He might have had second thoughts, people do.' *Like I'm having*, Marianne added to herself.

'There's the doorbell.' Mrs Gibb went to the window and lifted the curtain. 'I think this might be him, a taxi's just driven off. Do you want to answer it, Marianne?'

'Oh no, I can't, I'm in too much of a state!' Marianne wailed.

Renée took the bouquet from her and laid it on a small table. 'You're meeting your father, not having a tooth extracted. We'll go together.'

Marianne let Renée open the door while she stood behind, peering over her aunt's shoulder.

'Hello, Renée.'

'Hello, Jonny.' Renée pulled Marianne forward. 'Meet your daughter.'

Marianne held out her hand and the man on the doorstep shook it awkwardly.

'Pleased to meet you, and won't you step inside?' she offered, but she was so nervous her palms began to sweat. And she hardly dared look at him in case he had the dreaded Lacey widow's peak. But his hair was curly like hers, even though he'd tried to control it with Brilliantine. Fortunately he'd brushed it far enough off his forehead for her to see that there was no widow's peak to tarnish their relationship before it had even begun. How awful to have come all this way only to be told she wasn't his child.

But Renée wanted to keep things moving. 'I think we all need a drink,' she said, and guided Jonny into the breakfast room where she introduced him to Mrs Gibb, who had already poured them all a glass of her British sherry.

'Shall we toast the bride?' she suggested.

Jonny raised his glass and winked at Marianne; she relaxed slightly and smiled back.

'To my daughter. A beautiful bride.'

Yes, father and daughter, but strangers, and it's a bit weird meeting him for the first time on my wedding day. There was certainly some catching up to be done, nineteen years of it to be exact, if he hung around. For now that they'd met he could quite easily decide that having a daughter was a responsibility he could happily live without; he could walk out of her life as swiftly as he'd entered it. But not today, she hoped, because every girl should be given away by her father and, sitting there sipping sherry and chatting amiably to Mrs Gibb and Renée, he didn't look like a man about to make a run for it.

'Well, do I meet with your approval?' He smiled and Marianne blushed. She must have been staring.

'There's no doubt about your being father and daughter, there's a strong likeness,' Mrs Gibb answered.

Thank heaven for that, it had been confirmed, she wasn't a Lacey.

Mrs Gibb put down her glass. 'I think we should be on our way. Are you ready, dear?'

Marianne stood up and the magnitude of what she was about to embark upon hit her. Did she really want to be married, even to Franz, whom she loved dearly?

Her father moved over and tucked his arm through hers. 'Touch of nerves?'

Marianne nodded and Renée started fussing around, straightening her dress, dabbing a touch of powder on her nose, making sure that her veil and garland of flowers stayed put by anchoring them to her scalp with a whole packet of kirbi grips.

She was subjected to their critical gaze one last time, then Mrs Gibb placed the posy in her hand and her father led her out into the sunshine, and a happier future she hoped.

It was a short walk to the church and as they made their way along the road people came out of their cottages to wish her well. One small girl came running out and presented her with a horse-shoe for luck.

Gerald, Vealy and the two Gibb children danced along in front of them scattering rose petals. Knowing that her aunt and Mrs Gibb were responsible for these small touches, in a great wave of affection and gratitude Marianne stopped and hugged and kissed them both.

'What was that in aid of?' asked Renée.

'I haven't thanked you enough and you've both done such a lot for us.'

'I think she's telling you she's happy.' Jonny smiled and patted his daughter's hand.

'How could I be anything else? I arrived here thinking I was an orphan, and you don't know how lonely that feels. Nan was dead, Renée in America. She kept promising to come home, but I never saw her finding the money for the fare. But she did and gave me the surprise of my life when she turned up. It's a lot to take in.'

'And any minute now you will adding a third member to your family, a husband, and he's waiting for you now so I should put a step on it, duckie,' her aunt called.

'She's a lively one is Renée. Sylvie, your mum, was much quieter.'

'Who do I look most like, you or my mother?'

'Darling Sylvie. I was watching you in the house and it was eerie. She was beautiful, too.'

'You think I'm beautiful?' Marianne was astonished.

'I'll say. I loved Sylvie, you know, and although we were only kids, I still wanted to marry her, but your Nan forbade it. She hated the Ellis clan, particularly my dad, although I never worked out why. But I have to admit he was a bit of a rogue.

'But that doesn't matter now, and I'm just glad we've found each other. You don't know how much it means to me, and I'll be a good dad, I promise.'

But all Marianne could think about was the forthcoming wedding ceremony. Supposing she got into a muddle with all those words she had to repeat after the vicar? Trembling, she paused at the church doors and Doctor Gibb, who doubled up as church organist, burst into the *Wedding March*. The congregation rose and her father murmured, 'This is it.'

She could see Franz, but a great distance separated them. And she'd never make it down the aisle, not in these shoes with their heels and which were pinching like mad.

In a bit of a daze and hanging on to her father for dear life, Marianne made it. Franz smiled and her father handed her over to him. 'I love you,' Franz whispered and the marriage service began.

It was over; they were husband and wife. To soaring music they walked out of the church to be met by a hail of confetti. Wasting no time, Franz took his bride in his arms and, to a chorus of cheers and the delight of everyone, he kissed her. 'Hello, Mrs Hartmann.'

Still dazed by it all, Marianne stared down at her shining gold wedding ring. 'I can't believe it, we're really married.'

'We are, for ever and ever,' Franz confirmed and Marianne's arms slid round his neck.

'I'm so happy, and I do love you,' she murmured, resting her head against his chest.

'Can the bride and groom please turn and face me and stand still for a moment while I take a photograph,' Renée called, and with her camera, a posh American job, she snapped away: the bride and groom, then Marianne with her father, Daphne and Roger Gibb, their children, Gerald, even Boris, who'd somehow managed to get in on the act. Obediently they put on their best smiles.

Marianne had wondered how her father would react to Franz, but he was quite affable, shook his hand and said quietly, 'Look after my girl, I've just found her and as far as I'm concerned she's more precious than the crown jewels.'

It seemed to Marianne that the whole village had turned up to see their wedding and to wish them luck, but before they set off for the Gibb household, where they would cut the wedding cake that Mrs Gibb had made and sip her parsnip wine, Marianne had a task to perform.

'Ready girls? Here it comes,' she called and threw her posy into the crowd. Almost immediately there was an unladylike scramble from which Renée emerged triumphant, waving the small bouquet. Franz's best man, Marianne noticed, had made himself scarce.

And then somehow or other, the wedding party acquired a fiddler and Franz looked puzzled.

'Where has he come from?'

Marianne was as mystified as her new husband, especially when the fiddler took a place out in front and struck up a merry tune. Then, like the Pied Piper, he led them away from the Gibb house, where they were expected, towards the village green.

'Blimey.' Marianne and Franz stopped and stared in astonishment, for every tree had been draped with bunting and on a temporary wooden floor morris men were performing a dance which involved lots of bells and sticks. But what astonished everyone were the trestle-tables, groaning under the weight of pork pies, whole hams, huge joints of beef, pickles, beer, cider and lemonade. None of the villagers had seen such an abundance of food since before the war and they eyed it hungrily.

'Where does all this come from?' Puzzled, Marianne turned to Franz. 'We're not paying for it, are we?'

'No.' Franz laughed at the very idea.

'Maybe it was a good fairy.'

But then her father clapped his hands for silence. 'Ladies and gentlemen, what you see before you is my wedding gift to my daughter, Marianne, and my son-in-law, Franz. It is a celebration of their love for each other and I hope this will be just one of many memorable days in their married life. I would also like to invite the good folk of Stretton Magna to share in our happiness and partake of the feast. If you are wondering where all this meat is from, it's not black market, I had it sent over from southern Ireland where I have a farmer friend.'

There were loud cheers and some of the men were about to make a move in the direction of the beer table, when Jonny spoke again. 'Before the party begins in earnest I hope I can persuade the bride and groom to take to the floor for a waltz.'

Startled, Marianne looked up at Franz, but a man with an accordion began to play *The Blue Danube*. Franz gave a courtly bow, took his bride's hand and led her on to the floor. And as he swung her around and around, Marianne laughed for the pure joy of it. How can all these marvellous things be happening to me, a mere servant? In one day she'd married the most wonderful, most handsome man in the world and found her dad and it was hard to take it all in.

To start with people were shy about joining them on the floor, but gradually the small space filled with couples: Renée and the best man, Mr and Mrs Gibb, then Mr Veal and his wife, while the hungry and thirsty made a beeline for the laden tables.

Marianne and Franz danced until their feet were sore and their throats dry, then they found the shade of a tree. While Franz went to get something for them to drink, Marianne removed her sandals, rolled down her nylon stockings and buried her feet in the cool grass. Then she studied the villagers. Some of them were a little tipsy but enjoying themselves and it struck her how different their jovial sunburnt faces were from those she'd seen on that dark November night. Remembering it she shivered. The malevolent atmosphere: these same people but their features grotesque in the firelight, dancing to the single beat of a drum and chanting, 'burn the witch, burn the witch,' before throwing Anna's effigy into the flames. If she was only able to do one thing in this village, it would be to get the annual ritual burning of Anna stopped. Only then, she felt, would she be free of the ghosts.

'My darling wife, can we leave soon?' Franz murmured, coming up behind her and kissing her ear.

To calm herself, Marianne took a long drink of the cider Franz had brought her. This was the moment she'd been dreading, but could no longer avoid. Was she going to hate *it* and fail Franz? The whys and wherefores of marriage were a mystery to her and what she did know had been picked up from the women at the paper factory where she'd once worked. And she'd heard varying gruesome tales about the First Night, how it felt as though you were being ripped apart when he put his thing in yours, how you screamed from the pain, how you found yourself drenched in blood and how disgusting the whole business was. And another thing: if you'd done it before with some other bloke, well you had better yell blue murder to show you were still a virgin.

'Can we go?' Franz repeated.

'In a moment.' Marianne reached up and stroked his face. Surely her lovely, caring husband wasn't going to turn out to be some thoughtless rampaging beast? 'May we sit here in the shade a little longer so that I can finish this cider? I'm hungry too, and before we go I have to thank my dad for all he's done for us. It must have cost him a fortune.'

So while Franz went off to get his wife something to eat, Marianne looked for her dad so that she could thank him for his generosity. A young lady was showing him the steps of a folk dance and he looked rather merry.

'Dad,' she called. She waved, and he walked a trifle unsteadily towards her. 'Thank you for today, it's very generous of you and a real surprise. But how did you do all this without anyone finding out?'

'I phoned the pub, asked them if they could arrange something, got here last night and most of it was done while we were in church today marrying Franz.'

'I'll never be able to return such kindness.'

'Yes you can, by giving me lots of grandchildren. By the way, I've decided to get a job in Leicester so that I can watch them grow.'

But perhaps that wasn't the only reason, Marianne thought, as the young woman grabbed him by the arm and led him back to the dancers.

She was making her way across the green when Gerald, who'd been playing cowboys and Indians with his friends came racing across, overtook her and flopped down beside Franz.

'Enjoying yourself, young man?' said Franz.

Gerald picked at the grass. 'Why did you and Marianne have to go and marry each other?'

'Because we love each other.'

'Well, it's spoilt everything. What about me? Where am I going to live?'

'Your mother will want you with her now. After all this time you've got a lot of catching up to do.'

'She doesn't want me. She told me so yesterday when Doctor Gibb took me to visit her. She says she has no intention of living in any council house with lots of poor people.'

'So where does she plan to live?' asked Marianne.

'She said London, as soon as her inheritance comes through. She also said she doesn't want me with her because a boy of my age would cramp her style.'

Blimey, thought Marianne, there's a hard heart. And to think this was a woman she'd secretly admired, copied even.

'But she just can't leave you to cope on your own, it wouldn't be allowed.'

'She's going to find a foster home for me.' Gerald's voice began to quaver and he quickly wiped his eyes with the back of his hand. 'Nobody wants me.'

'Come here.' Marianne wrapped her arms around him and held him close. 'You will always have a home with us and maybe we could work something out, be your foster parents until you get your money.'

Gerald sat up. 'Could you really?'

'We might even be entitled to a council house.' She glanced at Franz. He was looking extremely fed up. 'We'll talk about it later; now off you go and play with your friends and don't forget you're staying with Dr Gibb and his family for a couple of nights.'

She'd been astonished when she heard that once the debts were settled, there would be some money left from the sale of Hope Grange. Even more astonishing was that Hugo Lacey had got round to making a will. The money was to be divided between Felicity and Gerald, Gerald's to remain in a trust until he was twenty-one.

Franz pulled Marianne to her feet with a very determined look on his face. 'We are going now and no one is stopping us.'

Marianne, who felt dizzy from the cider, giggled and Franz, a little angry at all these people wanting his wife's attention, kissed her hard to remind them that she was now his wife.

A glorious day was ending as they walked back to the cottage through fields of golden corn. Marianne was still wearing her wedding dress and her legs were brown and bare. Franz, happier now that they were alone, loosened his tie, removed his jacket and slung it over his shoulder. This was their first chance to be alone after a hectic day and they walked slowly, savouring the peace and their first few hours of marriage and stopping frequently to kiss. A moon was rising in the sky, bats darted around in the twilight and somewhere a nightingale began to sing. 'I think Mother Nature has laid this on especially for us,' said Franz as he gently lowered Marianne to the ground. After making a pillow for her with his jacket he began to undress. Marianne had never seen a naked man before so she watched him shyly. His body was muscular from hard work, the skin unblemished and brown from the sun. When he was naked, he undid the buttons on her dress and removed it. 'All day I've been thinking about this,' he murmured, kissing her breasts, their young bodies learning, exploring. Then with a mounting passion there was a joyous coming together. No pain, no blood, but a starburst of exquisite pleasure that consumed her body. Triumphant, exhausted they lay on their backs staring up at the sky.

Franz leaned over and kissed her gently, reverently. 'I think I have made you a happy lady.' He smiled. 'Shall we stay here or go back to the cottage?'

'Stay here.' Satiated, sleepy, Marianne rested her head on Franz's chest, closed her eyes and slept. It was dark when she woke and the sky was thick with stars. Franz was still asleep so she rolled on top of him and kissed him awake. This time there was no worrying about her modesty and afterwards they sang and danced naked in the moonlight. 'Do you think we might have made a baby?' Marianne asked as they fell away from each other.

'Maybe, but I would like a little time with you before we become parents.'

Dreamy, her body relaxed, Marianne said, 'I think I would like to go home now.'

The sky was streaked with red and the bird population of Leicestershire had burst into song. Standing at their front door, Marianne gave a small sigh. Would she ever again have the chance to be as happy as she had been this night? She doubted she ever would.

'I can see it, you're in the doldrums.' Franz studied her with concern. 'We must do something about it.' He picked her up, carried her across the threshold and up the stairs to their bedroom. And there, after they'd made love, they slept, locked in each other's arms, unaware that their beloved first-born son was already growing in his mother's womb and which, nine months hence, would give Marianne the second happiest day of her life.

NEATH PORT TALBOT LIBRARY
AND INFORMATION SERVICES

1		25		49		73	
2		26		50		74	
3		27		51		75	
4		28		52		76	
5		29		53		77	
6		30		54		78	
7		31		55		79	
8		32		56		80	
9		33		57		81	
10		34		58		82	
11		35		59		83	
12		36		60		84	
13		37		61		85	
14		38		62		86	
15		39		63		87	
16		40		64		88	
17		41		65		89	
18		42		66		90	
19		43		67		91	
20		44		68		92	
21		45		69		COMMUNITY SERVICES	
22		46		70			
23		47		71		NPT/111	
24		48		72